"There are so many great twists and turns in this short noir paperback... The writing is vivid and economical, and a lot happens ... leading up to the satisfying conclusion."
—*Paperback Warrior*

"Screams along like a '57 Plymouth with some nice twists and interesting characters, as a piano playing assassin plots a tough hit in a small upstate New York town. Top notch '50s Pulp Crime fiction."
—*GoodReads*

"It has all the necessary elements to make for a hard-boiled crime novel. Especially the femme fatale, in this case a 15-year-old girl, and a twist ending."
—Jeff Vorzimmer

"Steve Garrity, a mob hit man, is assigned to go to a small town and kill Leda Noland, who's only fifteen. He doesn't want the job, but he's not given any options. He's not told why he has to kill her, either, but he's told it has to look like an accident. He's given only a short time to go to the town, set up a cover, and make the hit. As you've probably guessed already, things do not go as planned."
—Bill Crider, *Pop Culture Magazine*

So Young, So Wicked

BY

Jonathan Craig

Black Gat Books • Eureka California

SO YOUNG, SO WICKED

Published by Black Gat Books
A division of Stark House Press
1315 H Street
Eureka, CA 95501, USA
griffinskye3@sbcglobal.net
www.starkhousepress.com

SO YOUNG, SO WICKED
Originally published in paperback by Gold Medal Books, Green-
wich, and copyright © 1957 by Fawcett Publications, Inc. Reprinted by permission of the agent for the estate.

ISBN-13: 978-1-951473-30-3

Book design by Jeff Vorzimmer, ¡caliente!design, Austin, Texas
Cover art by Barye Phillips from the 1960 reprint edition

PUBLISHER'S NOTE:
This is a work of fiction. Names, characters, places and incidents
are either the products of the author's imagination or used fiction-
ally, and any resemblance to actual persons, living or dead, events
or locales, is entirely coincidental.

First Stark House Press/Black Gat Edition: April 2021

CHAPTER ONE

Steve Garrity saw the burned paper match wedged between the door and the jamb an instant after he had inserted his key and started to twist the knob. He paused, abruptly and completely motionless, and suddenly the muggy August morning seemed chill. The match was a signal that Licardi had been here, a warning to stay in the apartment until he came again. And a visit from Licardi could have only one meaning.

He took a deep breath and reached for the match. Number nine, he thought as he bent it slowly between his thumb and forefinger. Number nine. Just a burned paper match stuck in a door, and yet it means that a man's going to die, and that I'm the one who's going to kill him.

He frowned at the match, flicked it away, and stepped into the apartment. Outside in the corridor the air had been stifling, heavy with the stored humidity of a night that had kept the air-conditioned club where Steve played piano filled with customers until closing time, at four A.M.—but here in the living room the air was dry and cool, kept that way around the clock by Steve's own air-conditioning unit in one of the huge front windows that faced the uptown side of East 51st Street. The apartment had four rooms, all of them expensively furnished, all of them soundproofed. Not even the rush-hour cacophony of midtown Manhattan penetrated here; the almost inaudible hum of the air-conditioning unit was the only sound.

He walked past the grand piano, past the low sectional sofa, past the hi-fi and the television console, and opened the doors of the cellaret. He rarely drank alone, but there were times when he felt an exception was in order, and this was one of them. He poured a pony of rye into a highball glass, filled the glass half-

way up with plain water, added an ice cube, and put
the drink down on top of the cellaret while he took
off his jacket and tie and opened his collar. Then he
picked up the glass, sipped at it slowly for a moment,
and walked back to the piano. He sat down before it,
took a deep swallow of his drink, and put the glass
down on the lowered top. It would be good for him if
he could get drunk, he thought. Just once. He'd like
to really hang one on. But there was no point in
thinking about it. Professional killers didn't get
drunk; if they were smart they didn't drink at all. Not
if they wanted to stay alive. One good drunk, and a
little—a very little—loose talk, and it would be all
over.

He played softly for a moment, trying to work a
little of the tenseness out of his arms and shoulders;
and then, suddenly, he brought all ten fingers down
viciously against the keys in a roaring discord, picked
up his glass, carried it out to the kitchen, and emptied
the rest of his drink into the sink.

The pattern was always the same, he reflected.
First there was the instant of fear, and then the minute or two of resentment, and finally the inevitable
resignation to the fact that you were going to murder
a man—for money, and because you had no choice. If
you didn't murder him, the syndicate would murder
you. It was as simple as that.

The door buzzer sounded just as he finished rins-
ing out the glass and setting it on the drainboard. He
walked back to the living room, fastened the night
chain in its slot, and opened the door the three inches
the chain permitted.

It was Licardi. Steve unhooked the chain and motioned him inside.

"You're a real careful boy," Licardi said, smiling.
"You open the door just wide enough for somebody
to stick a gun inside, and no more."

"I knew it'd be you," Steve said. "Who else

would it be? Hell, it's five o'clock in the morning."

"That's just the trouble," Licardi said. "Five o'clock's when a guy's brain starts to tire out on him. That's what happened in Cincinnati, ain't it? This guy opened the door for you a couple inches. It was enough, wasn't it? Sure. You want to make a man a drink, or do I fix it myself?"

"You know where it is," Steve said. "Fix it yourself."

Licardi shrugged and waddled toward the cellaret. He was a very short, very thick-bodied man with tremendous shoulders, close-cropped gray hair, and a fat, bulging neck that sweated constantly. His round face had a yellowish cast to it, and there were mud-brown streaks in the whites of his eyes. Just beneath his hair, and extending from one side of his forehead to the other, was a grayish band of skin almost an inch wide—the mark left, Steve had assumed, by an electric needle when a much younger and much vainer Licardi had had his hairline raised.

"Lousy liquor you've got," Licardi said as he stirred the drink. "You could afford better."

"I've got better," Steve said. "It's just that I save it for my friends."

Licardi grinned, walked to the sofa, and sat down heavily. Steve stared at him for a moment, then sat down on a hassock and lit a cigarette. "All right, Vince," he said. "Let's have it."

"Don't rush me," Licardi said. "This is one you ain't going to like."

"What makes you think I like any of them?"

Licardi glanced about the living room. "You live pretty good, Steve. Nice and cool in here. Nice and quiet, too. What'd this place rock you?"

"If you mean for the air-conditioner and the soundproofing, twenty-eight hundred."

Licardi nodded. "And the furniture?"

"Another grand and a half."

"Not counting the hi-fi and the piano, of course."

"For God's sake, Vince. What are you, a tax appraiser?"

"Like I said, you live pretty good. You asked me what made me think you like your work. That's why. Because it lets you live so good."

"Oh, sure. If I lived any better I couldn't stand it."

"Yeah."

"You going to keep this up all night?"

Licardi sighed. "All right, so rush me. Make me feel like I ain't wanted." He reached into his inside jacket pocket, took out a photograph about the size of a postcard, and sat studying it for a moment before he handed it to Steve.

"Nice, eh?" he said. "This kid was just fifteen last month. My God, think what she'll be like in about three years from now."

The photograph was of a small, almost incredibly pretty girl with a pomponed shako set at an angle on dark, shoulder-length hair, a fringed jacket that swelled tautly over upthrust breasts, and a snug hip-length skirt that reached the tops of her thighs and no farther. She had the smallest waist and the most nearly perfect legs Steve had ever seen.

"She's one of these drum majorettes," Licardi said.

"You're kidding," Steve said. He dropped the picture on the coffee table and looked at Licardi. "Go ahead, why don't you? Tell me you're getting next to that. I haven't had a decent laugh all night."

Licardi picked up the picture, held it close to his eyes, and shook his head slowly. "Jesus," he said softly.

"Watch yourself, Vince," Steve said. "You'll get the girl all wet."

"Man, she's really something, ain't she? Look at those legs. And only just turned fifteen. My God."

Steve made an impatient gesture with his cigarette. "Why don't you stop dreaming, Vince? You're never going to do anything about that, and you know it."

Licardi nodded, still looking at the picture. "No," he said. "But you are."

"Me? You crazy? I wouldn't fool around with anything that young for—" He broke off abruptly, staring at Licardi.

Licardi glanced at him over the top of the picture and smiled. "You're going to do something about her, all right, Steve. You're going to kill her."

"Kill a fifteen-year-old girl? Now I know you're crazy."

"What's the matter, boy?" Licardi said, his smile widening. "You a little squeamish about killing women?"

"You call that a woman? She's nothing but a kid."

"Yeah? Your eyes ain't good. Take another look at that build on her."

"To hell with the build. To hell with the whole idea. You must have gone out of your mind."

"Not me," Licardi said. "Me, I'd do damn near anything to her before I killed her. But it ain't me that does the deciding. I just get the word and pass it along to you, like always. And the word is that the kid's got to be hit. Get used to the idea, Stevie and get used to it fast."

"But she's—"

"But nothing. She's all yours, Steve."

Steve wet his lips. "But why me? Why didn't they pick someone else?"

"Because they didn't want nobody else," Licardi said. "All the other torpedoes look like just what they are. But you don't. You're a real handsome, clean-cut young guy that looks like he ought to be a salesman or something. You're the only one could get away with it."

"Bull," Steve said. "It's out, Vince. Tell them to get another boy."

"Sure," Vince said. "That's just what I'll tell them. I'll say you've decided to retire. Then all you'll have to do is guess where they'll give it to you—in the belly or in the head, or maybe both. They ain't cheap when it comes to using lead, Steve; that's one thing you got to hand them."

"The whole damn outfit must have gone nuts."

"Uh-uh," Licardi said. "They don't make mistakes, Steve; you know that. But I ain't saying I envy you. It's going to be the toughest one you ever handled. Just her being so young and beautiful will raise enough noise, God knows, but that ain't all." He paused. "She lives in this little town upstate, this Garrensville. That's where you got to hit her, Steve. Right in this stinking little town that's got only about five or six thousand people in it, and where every one of them keeps an eye on everybody else all the time."

Steve ground out his cigarette and crossed to the cellaret. "What do they want me to do? Commit suicide?"

"It'll be suicide, sure enough, if you flub it," Licardi said. "You'll be on your own right down the line, like always."

"Sure," Steve said bitterly. "Like always."

He took his time making his drink, furious with himself for having reacted in the way he had. What had he been trying to do, give Licardi the idea he'd gone soft?

That could be dangerous. Once the higher-ups had the slightest reason to think you'd lost your nerve, they got rid of you. You lasted just as long as your nerve held out and you didn't bungle. Let your nerve falter just a little, or bungle a job just a little, and the syndicate would make you wish for death a long time before they gave it to you.

He carried his drink back to the hassock and sat down.

"Let me see that picture again," he said casually.

He studied the girl's face for several moments and then handed the photograph back to Licardi. "All right," he said. "I could pick her out of ten thousand."

"You won't have to," Licardi said. "There aren't that many people in the whole town. And besides, there couldn't be more than one piece like that in the whole state, let alone a little jerk place like this Garrensville."

Licardi held the photograph by one corner, ignited the opposite corner with his cigarette lighter, and held it until the flame reached his fingers. Then he dropped it into the ash tray and poked at the curled ash with his forefinger.

"A damn wonder it didn't catch fire all by itself," he said. "What with the way that kid gives off heat and all."

"What's her name?" Steve asked.

"Leda," Licardi said. "Leda Louise Noland."

"What'd she do to rate a hit?"

"Don't ask foolish questions," Licardi said shortly. "What's the matter, you getting nose trouble?"

Steve shook his head. "A girl like that. I just don't get it, Vince."

"What's to get? All you got to worry about is seeing that she don't get any older."

Steve took a swallow of his drink and looked at the charred fragments in the ash tray. "Why all the sweat?" he said. "I've done jobs in small towns before, Vince."

"Not like this one, you ain't," Vince said. "This Leda's the town beauty, for God's sake. She's the kind just naturally gets all the attention there is around, anyhow. And now, ever since they threw her old man in the county clink, everybody keeps an eye on her harder than ever."

"What's he in for?"

"I don't know what for. He's in, and it ain't no skin off yours or mine. Anyhow, what with the kid's mother dead ever since she was born, and with her old man cooling it in jail, she comes in for a lot of notice. She's living with an aunt, a woman named Nancy Wilson. They're at Five-o-nine High Street. Got that?"

Steve nodded. "Five-o-nine High Street. Nancy Wilson."

"Just don't write it down anywhere," Licardi said. "Like I was telling you, what with all this attention she gets, you'll be lucky if you get her alone more'n five seconds before somebody starts wondering what in hell a sharp type like you is doing futzing around with her. That Garrensville ain't the big town, boy; they don't like it for grown men to futz around their little girls."

"Maybe you could line up a female torpedo somewhere. It'd be simpler all the way around."

"Don't crack wise."

"All right, so say it's only five seconds. How long do you think it takes to pull a trigger?"

Licardi grinned mirthlessly. "Hot, ain't it?"

"What?"

"This weather. It's cooked your brain."

"What's that supposed to mean?"

Licardi leaned forward, rested his elbows on his knees, and spoke with a voice that was strangely flat, almost toneless.

"I mean there ain't going to *be* any trigger," he said. "I mean there ain't going to be any gun, or any knife, or any ice pick, or any damn weapon at all."

Steve started to speak, then changed his mind and sat staring at Licardi unblinkingly.

"Don't bother asking me why," Licardi went on. "Just listen, and listen good. This hit's got to look like an accident. Hell, it's got to more than look like one; it's got to be one."

"Accident!"

"Yeah, accident. That's going to make it just about as dangerous as a hit can get. But that's the way it has to be, Steve; there's no way around it. If there was, the boys would take it. They don't fancy these things up just for the hell of it."

Steve lowered his glass to the coffee table, his eyes on Licardi's face. "Listen, Vince—"

"Don't 'Listen, Vince' me," Licardi said. "I ain't much higher up in this outfit than you are. All I do is bring you the word." He leaned back against the cushion and nodded slowly. "It has to look like an accident, Steve. You make it look like anything else, and you're a dead man."

"But how do they expect me to—"

"They don't care about how," Licardi said. "They leave that up to you."

"It's impossible."

"It better not be," Licardi said. "You know that much, if you don't know anything else."

Steve reached for his drink, brought it half to his mouth, then set it back down again. "It means I'd have to hang around and wait for a chance to phony something up. It might be days before I got a chance to pull it, even if I figured something out. It'd take a long time, maybe even weeks."

"Not weeks," Licardi said. "A few *days* you've got, yes. But that's all. You'll have to work up some kind of cover for being there, too. And you'll have to stay around for a while after the hit. You can't just scratch her and take off; they'd have you pegged for the job ten minutes after they found out you'd left. You've got to have a damn good reason to be there in the first place, and you've got to hang around and mingle with the folks a while afterward."

"That's all?" Steve said. "You sure that's all,

Vince?"

"It's tough, I admit."

"What's tough about it? All I have to do is go to
a town where I'll stand out like a man from Mars and
somehow get to a girl that everybody in the place is
watching over every minute of the time, and then just
more or less see to it that she has an accident that
kills her. If that's all I have to do, why'd you try to
make it sound so tough for?"

"Don't be bitter," Licardi said. "You're getting
paid, ain't you?"

"Yes, but not enough. No amount would be
enough for a job like that."

"And on the other hand," Licardi said, "if you
don't do it, you end up dead. This way, you at least
got a chance."

Steve said nothing. It always came back to that,
he thought; you never had a choice.

"It'll be three grand this time," Licardi said.
"C.O.D., of course. That's a grand more'n you ever
got before."

"Great," Steve said. "C.O.D. Just great."

"Don't forget, if the boys wanted to, they
wouldn't have to pay you a lousy dime. A lot you've
got to holler about."

"Yeah. A lot."

Licardi smiled. "By the way, I heard you the other night. You got a nice way with a piano, boy. I like
it."

"Thanks," Steve said. "That makes me feel a lot
better."

"I was out in the bar," Licardi said. "You
couldn't see me. But I like the way you make it, no
kidding. You play a real nice piano."

"Thanks again."

"Maybe too nice. Anyway, too nice for that little
dive you work in. Maybe you're getting ideas about
moving over to the East Side, to one of those fancy

places that drag the tourist trade."

"Stop backing up to it, Vince. What are you getting at?"

"The boys figure you should stay right where you are. That little neighborhood restaurant don't draw no out-of-towners at all."

"So?"

"Well, if you started working in some of those East Side traps, you'd be sitting up there for all the out-of-towners to look at. And sooner or later it just might happen that one of them might remember seeing you back in his home town."

"Forget it, Vince. There were never any witnesses."

"Maybe, and then again maybe there were. Anyhow, the word is that—"

"I said forget it. I won't ever be playing any of those places, Vince. I'm not even in that league."

"No? Well, you sounded pretty good to me. Just good enough to wonder about."

"Knock it off, will you, Vince? I've got to think."

Licardi nodded. "You're a guy with something to think about, I admit." He finished his drink and got to his feet. "Well, you've got one nice break, anyhow. This is summertime, so the kid won't be in school. If she was in school every day, it might get complicated."

"You're funny as hell, Vince."

"Yeah. You got everything straight now?"

"It's a breeze."

"Still bitter, eh? Look at it this way, Steve: Figure it's a challenge."

"Go to hell."

Licardi laughed, took his wallet from his pocket, and counted out five hundred dollars in twenty-dollar bills. "Expense money," he said. "Take it easy and you ought to come out a few hundred to the good." He waved a hand at Steve and crossed to the door.

"Wait a minute," Steve said. "Suppose I want to get in touch with you."

Licardi paused, his hand on the knob. "You mean like in an emergency?"

"Yes. How do I reach you?"

Licardi shook his head. "You don't. Once I walk out this door, you're on your own. Strictly."

"But—"

"Uh-uh," Licardi said. "There won't be any emergencies, Stevie. You're going to see to that." He smiled. "That's the only way you keep on breathing."

Chapter Two

For several minutes after Licardi had left the apartment Steve sat very still, staring at the sheaf of twenty-dollar bills without quite seeing them, his drink long since forgotten.

Licardi had put it to him squarely: From this moment on he was strictly on his own. He'd been given an almost impossible assignment, one that couldn't conceivably have been more dangerous, and he had to carry it out alone.

They'd left it entirely up to him. If he didn't go through with it, he'd be killed by the syndicate. If he did go through with it and bungled, he would be killed just the same. If he got caught at it, he'd go to the chair. And if he went to the chair, he would still be on his own. He wouldn't be able to take anyone else with him; he wouldn't even be able to put anyone else in prison. The syndicate had made certain of that by limiting his contacts with it to just one man: Licardi.

And Licardi? Who was he? He was a man whom he'd never seen or talked to in any place other than his own apartment. And of course his name wasn't really Vincent Licardi at all; it couldn't have been. All he'd ever be able to tell the police was that his contact went by that name; and then, when the police looked through their records, there'd be no such names at all. And even if they started him through the mug books, and he came across Licardi's picture—what then?

Nothing. He couldn't prove a thing. He couldn't even prove that he hadn't picked Licardi's picture out arbitrarily, just to stall for a little time, just for a respite in the grilling.

He was a piecework employee of the syndicate, but when you came right down to it, he knew nothing at all about it except that it existed; and that much was common knowledge anyhow. He was a professional assassin, working for a national, perhaps international, association of criminals whose only concrete reality so far as Steve was concerned was embodied in a short, fat man with a sweating neck whom he knew as Vincent Licardi. Steve had read all the books, of course—the books exposing The Syndicate, or The Combination, or The Crime Cartel, or The Black Hand, or The Maffia—but most of the books and articles had contradicted one another and he'd wondered whether almost all of what he'd read wasn't sheer surmise and conjecture.

He'd read a lot, and he'd heard a lot—but he knew nothing.

But he worked for it, just as he would always work for it, as long as he lived. He was a hired killer, a torpedo, and he was one because he'd killed a man one night in sheer fury, and, just a few minutes later, been forced to kill a second man to avoid paying the penalty for the first.

And there was only Vincent Licardi between him and the men who passed out the death sentences; it had been that way since that first night when he'd killed two men and learned that the syndicate was real, that it had representatives everywhere and on every level—even in that tiny Missouri town west of St. Louis where he'd learned that any man is capable of anything, and where he'd discovered that almost all of what he had always thought of as his natural horror of committing murder was in fact only a fear of paying the price for it.

Now, almost two years after that first terrible night in Missouri, he could kill without remorse, without conscience-ridden nights, without experiencing anything at all beyond his intensified alertness before a hit and the almost euphoric afterglow when he was sure he'd got away with murder and that his life was still his own.

That was the surprising thing, the almost unbelievable thing: to learn that killing another man could mean so little, that it could, in fact, mean nothing more than a heightened awareness of what his own life meant to him.

Steve reached for his drink, but it tasted flat and he put it back down again. He was trying to concentrate on the job before him, but his mind kept wrenching back to that night in Missouri, the night it had all begun.

It had been a rainy night and the band had just finished the twentieth in a series of one-night stands that had taken it from New Orleans to St. Louis and was now taking it slowly west toward Kansas City. They'd been booked to open the town's new dance hall, but the wind and rain had begun early in the evening and the crowd had been very poor. Steve, with no instrument to pack and carry, had wandered away from the other musicians, walking aimlessly in the rain, killing time until the bus left for the next town and the next one-night stand.

On a street corner four blocks away from the hall he had passed a man with his chin tucked down into the front of his raincoat and a sodden hat pulled low over his eyes, shouldering through the rain with his gaze on the sidewalk. The other man hadn't even glanced at Steve, but Steve had recognized him instantly. He would, he had reminded himself often enough, have recognized Johnny Callan in hell.

Eight months before, when Steve had been playing as a single in St. Louis, he had come home to find his lovely new wife and Johnny Callan naked together on the studio couch. It had taken him a long moment to believe what he saw, and in that moment Callan had dived at him and knocked him to the floor. Steve had been too stunned to defend himself properly, and while he fought with Callan, his wife had stood above them, all pink and white and soft in her nakedness, with a look on her face that he had never seen on a woman's face before.

It was his wife who had kicked him in the temple and given Callan a chance to get to his feet. And then Callan had taken over. He had kicked Steve more times than Steve could remember, and each kick had been squarely in the groin.

Then, while Steve lay helpless, so paralyzed with pain that he couldn't move, his wife and Callan had laughed, and dressed, and left him there.

He had spent six days in the hospital, and another eight days looking for his wife and Callan; then he had drifted south, playing for whatever he could get in one bar after another, until he reached New Orleans.

Now, when he recognized Callan, he paused, glanced both ways along the deserted street, and fell into step behind him. When they came to an alley, he closed the distance between them and drove his fist into the base of Callan's spine. Callan gasped and fell against the brick wall of the alley, and Steve hit him again, this time in the pit of the stomach. Then he dragged Callan into the alley and began, slowly and methodically, with no regard for his hands, to beat him to death. Once, when he felt certain Callan must be dead, he paused and listened to his heart. It was still beating, though very slowly. He took off his necktie, wrapped it around the knuckles of one hand, wrapped his handkerchief around the knuckles of the other, and went back to work.

At last he had finished and started to rise to his feet.

"Easy, now," a voice said, and Steve whirled around to face a uniformed cop with a gun in his hand.

Steve's first reaction was disbelief—the same kind of disbelief he had experienced when he walked in on his wife and Johnny Callan. And then came panic, and a sudden, belly-twisting nausea that left him so weak he was forced to lean against the wall for support.

The cop kept both his gaze and his gun on Steve while he knelt beside Callan's body. When he straightened up again there was something close to a smile on his face.

"Buddy of yours?" he asked, almost conversationally.

Steve said nothing.

"I haven't seen you around before," the cop said. "Stranger in town." He studied Steve's face for a moment, then glanced down at Callan's body and nudged it with the toe of his shoe. "And him, too—judging from what little you left of his face. Damn. You sure did a good job on him, mister; I'll have to say that for you."

The next two hours seemed more like nightmare than reality. The cop led Steve to a cruiser parked at the far end of the alley and handcuffed him to a metal bar in the back seat. Twenty minutes later Steve had been questioned briefly by a detective, put in a cell, and left alone.

A few minutes later he had had a visitor, an aging, stoop-shouldered man with a dark, heavy-featured face, eyes like polished onyx, and a soft whispery voice that sounded as if someone had once struck him across the throat with a rubber hose.

The man said very little, but it was enough. Steve had a choice: He could go to the Missouri gas chamber for murdering Johnny Callan—or he could kill still another man as a favor to the man with the whispery voice. He could die for one murder, or go free for two, it was as simple as that. The second murder would cancel out the first.

He hadn't understood it fully then, and it was only after he had gone back to New York that he discovered he had been talking to a member of the syndicate. At the time, he couldn't think beyond the gas chamber; all he could do was nod his head dumbly, listen to a few hoarse words of instruction, and try to keep from vomiting on the dirty cement floor of his cell.

The man with the whispery voice left, and a minute or so later the detective returned, grinned at Steve knowingly, and took him out a side entrance to a small panel truck parked a few yards down the street.

The detective said nothing until they reached the open countryside; then he handed Steve a revolver and four loose shells.

"Don't load it till you get out of the truck," he said. "And throw it away as soon as you get through. There ain't anybody ever going to trace it, and that's for sure."

As they approached a roadhouse on the other side of the road, the detective nodded toward it and then drove off onto the shoulder and parked in the deep shadows beneath a heavy stand of trees.

"You got everything clear in your mind now?" he asked.

Steve nodded. "Sure. And when I come back out again, you'll arrest me for this murder too."

"Trusting bastard, aren't you? Relax, son. This is a business deal, pure and simple."

"If it's so simple, why are you dragging me in on

it?"

"You ask too many questions, son. A man in your position shouldn't set up so much of a holler. Now if you'd rather catch a couple lungfuls of that Jeff City gas, just say so." He paused, his grin wide. "I thought so. Okay, so get out. And listen, fella. Make sure you don't get no ideas. If you do, I just might have to shoot the pure hell out of you."

"You will, anyway."

"Nah. That ain't in my orders. Get going."

Steve climbed out of the truck, watched it move away, and then loaded the revolver and started across the macadam to the roadhouse. He hadn't been aware that another car had been following them, but now he saw it draw to a stop a few yards behind him. Four men got out, ran rapidly in the direction of the road-house, split up into pairs, and disappeared in the trees at either side of it. They were there to make sure he went through with this, Steve realized, and they would probably be waiting to kill him the instant he came out.

But almost no chance at all was still better than none, and Steve hesitated only long enough to fix the position of the place where the detective had told him he would be waiting for him. Then he crossed the wide gravel apron to the entrance and picked his way through the crowd to the bar. When his drink had been served, he walked back to the men's room, forcing himself not to look at anyone.

He walked past the men's room and opened the door just beyond it—the door the whispery voice had told him about—and moved along a short corridor to still another door. He stood motionless, listening, but there was no sound of voices beyond the door, nothing to indicate his intended victim was not alone.

Then he raised the gun, jerked the door open, and fired four times at the white-haired man behind the desk directly opposite the doorway.

A moment later he had run to the far end of the corridor, opened the door that led out into the night, and was racing through the trees toward the panel truck. The detective already had the motor running, and he had the truck in gear and moving away almost before Steve had jumped inside.

"Hell of a rain tonight," the detective said. "Been like this for near a month, off and on." He took a handkerchief from his pocket and wiped the windshield with it, whistling softly under his breath. "Sure steams up, don't it?"

"Why?" Steve asked, letting the one word stand for all the questions.

The detective shrugged. "Don't ask me, fella. I just do what they tell me. Maybe Whitey just plain talked too much. Maybe it would have been hard for somebody he knew to get past the guys he's got scattered around the place. I dunno." He drove as if he enjoyed it, his body slouched comfortably in the seat. "You toss the gun, like I told you?"

"No," Steve said, reaching into his waistband. "I—"

"No harm done," the detective said. "A fella can't think of everything. Just kind of give her a heave over there in those trees. It don't matter who finds it, long's they don't find it on you or me."

Steve threw the gun as far as he could and then sat on the edge of the seat, his body rigid. "What now?" he asked.

The detective turned his head to stare at him blankly for a moment. "What's the matter? You still worried?"

"I mean what happens when we get back to town?"

"Nothing much at all. I just let you out on a dark street somewhere and you just sort of amble on back to the bus station. Of course, if you figured you'd had enough of that music business and you was thinking of settling down somewhere, we'd be real glad to have you. We've got a mighty friendly little town, for a fact."

Steve watched the shadowy forms of the trees racing past the window and said nothing.

After the detective had let him out of the truck, Steve walked to the bus station and went into the men's room to examine his hands. His knuckles were bruised and swollen and the skin above them was raw, scraped away by the blows to Johnny Callan's face, but they would be all right. He held his hands under the hot water faucet for several minutes, then shoved them into the pockets of his raincoat and went back out to the waiting room. The westbound bus he should have taken with the other members of the band had left almost an hour ago. He would be fired, he knew. Not that it made any difference. He wouldn't be able to play a piano for at least a week, and possibly longer.

He took his suitcases from the coin locker where he had stored them and bought a ticket on the next bus to St. Louis. In St. Louis he changed to a plane for New York. And it was during that long flight that he came to know himself, to realize that the horror he'd always felt at the thought of killing someone had been very little more than the fear of being caught and executed.

A month later, once his hands had healed and he had begun working steadily again, he found it possible to forget that night in Missouri for hours at a time; when he thought of it at all, he remembered only his panic when he'd heard the cop's voice behind him in the alley, and the terrifying minutes he'd spent alone in his cell thinking about the Missouri gas chamber.

Then one dawn Vincent Licardi had come calling. Licardi knew all about that night in Missouri, and he explained with a kind of amused patience just why it was that Steve was going to work for the syndicate, whenever and wherever it wanted to use him.

"You're working for us already," Licardi had said. "You did so good the first time, the boys decided to take you on permanent. You'll make 'em a good man. You got no record anywhere, and you got a perfect cover with your piano playing, and you don't look like no torpedo anybody ever saw before."

When Steve had tried to protest, Licardi had reminded him that both of the Missouri murders were still unsolved—and would remain unsolved so long as Steve continued to use his head.

"Not that the boys would go to all that trouble," Licardi had added. "They'd probably just sick some other torpedo onto you. Those murder raps are just a little extra inducement, in case you don't induce easy." He'd smiled. "Get used to the idea, boy. You're on the payroll, beginning now."

That was the way it had come about, the way in which Steve Garrity, professional pianist, had become Steve Garrity, professional pianist and killer.

And now, Steve reflected as he pocketed the money Licardi had left for him, the career that had begun in a little town in Missouri was almost certainly going to end in a little town in New York. The syndicate had given him an assignment that was the blood brother to suicide.

Steve rose, picked up the dirty glasses, and walked out to the kitchen. The clock on the wall over the stove said six-twenty; if he hurried, he could be in Garrensville before noon.

He drank a glass of orange juice, made a cup of instant coffee, and sat down at the table to work out a plan.

But it was no good; by the time he had finished his first cup and started on a second, he had resigned himself to the impossibility of making any plan at all until he was actually on the scene. Always before he had been furnished with considerable information, and he had supplemented it himself in every available way. He had looked for useful habits and weaknesses, and he had sometimes known almost as much about a victim as the victim knew about himself. And except for that first murder in Missouri, all his hits had been made in large cities; most of them in the Middle West and on the West Coast, none of them in New York.

That was another thing, he reflected: Garrensville was much too close to home. Damn it, they'd really stacked the deck this time. Not one thing about this hit was right. Not one thing was the way it had been on any of the others. The odds on getting away with the murder of a beautiful teen-aged girl in a town like Garrensville were just about the same as they were for drawing a straight flush.

He pushed back his chair and strode out to the bathroom. All he could do was go to Garrensville, size up the situation and Leda Noland, and take it from there. Until he knew everything there was to know about her, he wouldn't be able to devise a way for her to have her accident.

But she'll have it, he thought, as he turned on the cold water in the shower stall. She'll have it, one way or another. It's either her or me.

He stepped into the shower and bent his head so that the icy jet hammered at the back of his neck.

There wasn't any question that she would have an accident, none at all.

But how? he asked himself. How do I go about it?

CHAPTER THREE

By the time Steve had finished packing a bag, it was a quarter past seven. He had no close friends, either male or female; there was no one to account to except the manager of the club where he played and the part-time maid who came in on Mondays, Wednesdays, and Fridays. He left the maid a note saying he'd be away for a few days, folded it around one of Licardi's twenty-dollar bills, and left it on top of the cellaret. Then, because it was still much too early to phone the manager of the club, he called Western Union and dictated a telegram explaining that he had been called out of town by an emergency and suggesting the name of another pianist whom the manager might care to hire as a temporary replacement. He asked the operator to make sure the telegram was not delivered before eleven A.M., and then turned off the lights and the air-conditioner and went down to get his car from the garage.

He'd never taken his car on a hit before, but this time was different; this time, a car would be indispensable. No matter what plans he might make in Garrensville, he'd almost certainly need a car to carry them out. And besides, a man in a car would attract much less attention than a man afoot. The car itself was a last year's black Ford sedan, a car that would be almost as anonymous in Leda Noland's small home town as it was in New York.

At the garage, he asked for a map of New York State and studied it while the attendant was filling the tank. He wouldn't have to look at it again; the long years of memorizing piano scores at sight had left him with a mental photograph of the route to Garrensville that was almost as detailed as the map itself. As he eased the car out into the rush-hour traffic, he put the map in the glove compartment and glanced at his watch. It was exactly eight o'clock.

At a few minutes past eleven, Steve topped a small rise, dipped down again, rounded a curve, and suddenly he was in Garrensville. The town began abruptly, without the usual scattering of motels and service stations and outlying shacks. Steve had turned off the main highway several miles back, and the

vineyards and dairy farms he had passed on the way
had led him to expect Garrensville to be pretty much
like any of a hundred other upstate New York towns
he had been in.

It was not. It was much more like a small town in
the South. The highway became the main street and
ran along the east side of a town square that was
large enough to have accommodated a courthouse
had this been the county seat. Instead, the square held
only a statue of an Indian warrior on horseback,
whitened by pigeons and shading his eyes against the
sun as he reached into his quiver for an arrow.

There were several younger people paired off on
the green around the statue, and rows of old men
sunning themselves on the wooden benches that bordered the square on all four sides. The young girls
wore their hair longer here than the girls in New
York wore theirs, and most of the young men wore
white dress shirts with the collars open and the
sleeves rolled up just short of their elbows. A strong
breeze, sweet with the smell of a brush fire back in
the hills, stirred the girls' hair and picked at the skirts
of their thin summer dresses.

Steve drove slowly around the square, noting the
layout of the stores and shops and hotels. There were
two hotels, facing each other across the square. He
found a parking space near the more likely-looking of
the two, got his bag out of the back seat, and went
inside.

The lobby held half a dozen wicker chairs, a low
table with a welter of magazines on it, a cigarette machine shoulder to shoulder with a Coca-Cola machine, and a desk hardly wide enough to accommo-
date the extremely fat woman behind it. Steve walked
the three steps to the desk, put his bag on the floor,
and smiled at the clerk.

The clerk didn't smile back. She had a face so
heavily layered with fat that her features had lost all

definition, and her eyes were like dull brown stones at the backs of fleshy caves. A table radio at her elbow poured out a hillbilly ballad that made Steve wince, and above her head an old-fashioned ceiling fan creaked noisily without seeming to move the air at all.

"Yes?" she said.

"I'd like a room," Steve said. "A front one, if you've got it."

"We haven't. It's the back or nothing."

"All right."

The woman frowned. "For the night?"

"For a few days," Steve said. "I don't know just how long."

She shrugged and pushed a registration card toward him. "That's with bath. You want a radio, it's a quarter a day more."

Steve reached for the desk pen and started to sign the card. The pen was dry. He looked at the woman questioningly, but she was drumming her fingertips on the desktop, not looking at him. He took out his fountain pen and signed the card, using his real name and address. This was one time when an alias was not in order. If he made Leda Noland's death look like an accident, he had nothing to worry about, whether he used his real name or not. But if he should in some way arouse suspicion at any time before the accident or after it, a check on him would reveal the alias and trip him up. He would get away with Leda's murder either completely or not at all.

The woman took the registration card, frowned at it, and pushed it to one side. "Ollie!" she called loudly, and reached into the mail rack behind her for a key. "Telephone calls are fifteen cents," she said as she put the key on the desk. "This is a quiet place. See that you help us keep it that way."

Steve nodded. "I'm glad to hear it," he said. "I like a quiet place myself."

The woman turned the music up a little louder

and said nothing. A moment later an elderly man in a bellhop's uniform came along the corridor, scooped the key off the desk, picked up Steve's bag, and started back down the corridor without a word.

"Ice water in Four-o-six, Ollie," the woman said. "This is the second time I told you."

The old man muttered something under his breath and started up the stairs. He had sparse gray hair and tired rheumy eyes and almost no chin at all.

"No elevator?" Steve said.

"Christ, no. But you're lucky; you're only on the second."

"Nice break for me," Steve said. He reached out and took his bag from the old man's hand. "Let me, Ollie," he said. "She can't see you from here."

"Thanks," Ollie said. "They get heavier all the time." He led Steve along the second-floor hallway to the last door on the left. "Lucky you got a back room," he said, inserting the key. "This way you don't get all the racket from the street. Gets pretty noisy out there."

"I hadn't noticed," Steve said.

"Uh-huh. Well, maybe not too noisy for folks from New York. I guess you must be pretty used to it."

Steve grinned, making it friendly. "How'd you know I was from New York?"

"The clothes, mostly," Ollie said as he opened the door. "Those skinny lapels, for instance, and those pants without hardly any cloth in the legs."

"That's unusual?" Steve said as he stepped into the room.

"Around here it is," Ollie said. "Around here, even a man wearing a coat in the middle of the day is unusual."

Steve dropped his bag on the bed and crossed the room to open the window.

"I would have done that for you," Ollie said, not

moving from the doorway.

Steve fished in his pocket for a coin, then changed his mind and took out his wallet. He handed Ollie a dollar bill, watched the surprise that crossed his face, and grinned. "Thanks, Ollie," he said. "The room's fine."

Ollie closed the door and stood staring at the bill for a long moment; then turned it over and looked at the back, looked at the front of it again, and finally folded it carefully and tucked it into his pocket.

"Don't mention it," he said. "Anything I can do for you, just holler."

"I'll do that," Steve said. "Nice town you've got here, Ollie. I think I'm going to like it." Might as well start laying the groundwork right now, he decided, and keep sifting in bits of it as he went along.

"Yes," Ollie said, "it's a right nice little town. You thinking of staying a while, are you?"

Steve sat down on the side of the bed and crossed his legs. "I might," he said, smiling. "It depends on how things work out."

"Oh. You a businessman?"

"In a way," Steve said. "I'm just looking around, you might say."

Ollie nodded solemnly. "I see. Well, I wish you luck. This isn't much of a town for business, though. It's mostly grape and dairy country around here—but then, I guess you know that already."

"Maybe the town needs a little new blood."

"Well, I don't know," Ollie said. "Everybody used to do pretty good. But when they built that new highway they sort of by-passed us. Ever since then the town's been more or less dying on its feet."

"You wouldn't know it to look at it," Steve said.

"I don't believe I caught your name."

"Garrity," Steve said. "Steve Garrity."

Ollie grinned toothlessly. "Well, it's mighty good having you with us, Mr. Garrity. We don't get many folks from New York, but when we do we try to make them glad they came."

"I can see that already," Steve said.

"I guess you noticed we've got some right pretty girls around here."

"Yes, I did."

"That's just about all we have got—cows and grapes and pretty girls." He lowered his voice and stared at the wall behind Steve's head. "Maybe you might get a little lonesome, or a little thirsty sometime. If you do, you let me know."

Steve nodded. It was always the same, he thought. They put it a little differently here, but the routine was the same. "I'll keep it in mind, Ollie," he said. "I'm glad I know where to go."

"Any time," Ollie said. "But watch out for that old tub of lard downstairs. Mrs. Conklin. She can outbitch any other woman I ever heard of. Her old man run off with some little twitch-butt gal about four years ago, and Mrs. Conklin, she's been taking it out on people ever since. She just naturally hates everybody, men and women both."

"I see," Steve said. "I wondered what was wrong with her."

"So does everybody else, when they first meet her. They figure there must be something wrong with *them*. But don't let her throw you. You just ask for old Ollie; I'll take care of you good. No use in a man being lonely or thirsty unless he wants to, I always say."

"That's right," Steve said.

"Well, you let me know," Ollie said. He opened the door, winked a watery eye at Steve, and stepped out into the hallway.

Steve's smile went away at the same instant the door closed. He rose, walked to the window again, and pushed the curtain aside. The window opened on a wide parking lot between what appeared to be a supermarket and an automobile appliance store. Across the street from the parking lot was a row of one- and two-story homes, almost all of them painted white, with well-tended front lawns and vine-covered porches. There were children playing on the side- walks, and almost no automobiles on the street at all.

Steve dropped the curtain and glanced about the room. It was just another hotel room, exactly like any of a hundred others he'd stayed at in the years he'd toured with bands. Hotel rooms and bellhops were all the same, he reflected: No matter how much every- thing else might change from town to town and from one part of the country to another, the interiors of hotel rooms and the ways of bellhops never surprised you.

He draped his jacket over the back of the straight chair beside the writing desk, loosened his tie, and began to unpack his bag. I wonder what Ollie's face would have looked like if I'd told him I'd just stopped by to knock off the town beauty, he thought. Cows and grapes and pretty girls—my God.

When he had finished unpacking he sat down on the bed and slipped the Garrensville telephone direc- tory from beneath the Gideon Bible on the night stand. Vince Licardi had said that Leda was staying with an aunt named Nancy Wilson. He ran a thumb- nail down the list of Wilsons until he located "Wil- son, Nancy C." The address was the same as the one Licardi had given him. He started to close the directo- ry, but something had caught his eye and he flipped it open again.

The second listing in the Wilson column was the Wilson Gift Shop, 239 Main Street, and beneath the business number was an entry reading: "If no answer, call GA 4781."

He had been right; GA 4781 was the same num- ber he had seen listed after "Wilson, Nancy C."

Steve smiled and replaced the directory beneath

the Bible. This was a break. The fact that Leda's aunt Nancy was the proprietor of a gift shop meant that even a stranger like Steve could walk into the shop and start talking to her without arousing anyone's curiosity. It meant that Steve could start getting a line on Leda Noland right away. It was a place to start, and a person to start with, and from that point on he could play it by ear. And school was out, which meant there was even a possibility that Leda might be helping her aunt out in the shop.

Steve shook his head. No, he thought; it's a big enough break as it is. Having the kid working in the shop for the summer would be too much to hope for. Let's not be greedy, Steve; the next thing you know, you'll be having her fall down the cellar steps and break her gorgeous little neck for you, just as a favor.

But what kind of cover story ought he to use with the kind of woman Leda's aunt Nancy was likely to be? Hell, he didn't need one. Not yet. The thing to do was walk into the shop and look around, just the way anyone else might do, and then make with the lip a little and see what developed. Just play it by ear, that's all. If Aunt Nancy was proud of her niece, as was probably the case, it should be easy to start her talking about her.

He got up from the bed, put on his coat, and glanced at his watch. It was half past twelve, a time when the gift shop was likely to be crowded with lunch-hour shoppers. But that was all right, too; he could look the town over for a while, and then wander into the shop a few minutes after one. And now that he thought about it, he was very hungry. He'd had nothing but orange juice and coffee since yesterday evening, and it would be better to eat now, while he waited for Nancy Wilson's customers to thin out.

In the lobby, he dropped his key on the desk, smiled pleasantly at the scowling Mrs. Conklin, and stepped out onto the sidewalk.

The same young couples were still on the green around the statue in the square, the same old men were still sunning themselves on the benches, and the Indian brave was still trying to pluck an arrow from his quiver. Steve hesitated for a moment, then walked west, looking for a restaurant.

There were more people on the sidewalks now than there had been when he checked into the hotel, but no one seemed to pay any particular attention to him. Occasionally a young girl would glance at him guardedly, and once a very pretty middle-aged woman walking with a man smiled at him openly, but that was all. He was struck again by the similarity between Garrensville and the small towns he had known in the South. It was an easygoing town, almost a lazy town, and the pace was slow. The people here didn't rush along the sidewalks, the way he had begun to do the moment he left the hotel, and the snatches of conversation he overheard were relaxed, completely unhurried. He slowed his own steps for a few yards, then wondered what difference it could make, and quickened his pace again.

He stopped at the first restaurant he came to, paused a moment to glance at the menu posted by the door, and went inside. He had a small steak with a baked potato and tossed salad, and finished the meal with black coffee and brandy. He would have preferred espresso, but he knew it would have been a waste of time to ask for it; the waitress had even done a double take when he'd asked for brandy.

He lingered over his coffee until a quarter past one, then crossed the square and walked along Main Street, looking for the number of Nancy Wilson's gift shop.

He found it in the block beyond the square, a very narrow one-story building that looked as if it might once have been intended as a private residence. The show window was filmed with dirt and the gifts

on display behind it looked as if they hadn't been
dusted in a long time. On the door, between the glass
and the drawn shade, was a hand-lettered sign that
read: THIS FINE LOCATION FOR RENT OR
SALE—CALL GA 4781.

Steve stood there for a long moment, frowning at
Nancy Wilson's home phone number; then, suddenly,
his frown disappeared.

Nancy Wilson's going out of business hadn't
changed anything, he realized. In fact, it was all to the
good. He could still talk to her without arousing suspicion, and there was even a better chance of meeting
Leda at her aunt's home than there would have been
at her gift shop.

But the really important thing was that he no
longer had to worry about a cover story. He had one,
and it was very nearly perfect.

Chapter Four

It was a neighborhood of small, very old houses,
wide front lawns, and ornamental shrubbery. There
were huge trees behind most of the houses and along
the curbs, and even in midafternoon High Street was
in deep shade, the air heavy with the scent of flower
gardens and freshly cut grass.

Steve parked in front of 509, followed the winding flagstone walk to the front porch, and rang the
bell. There was a metallic creaking sound to his left,
and he turned.

He had seen the porch glider before he rang the
bell, but it faced away from the door and the girl had
been lying down in it, hidden by the back. She rose,
smoothed the hair away from her forehead, and came
toward him.

"I must have fallen asleep," she said, smiling ten-
tatively. "I was reading."

She was about twenty-six, Steve judged, a slim,

auburn-haired girl with widely spaced gray eyes, a small blunt nose, and very white skin. Her hair was thick and slightly mussed, and she wore no make-up whatever.

"Sorry I woke you," Steve said.

"That's all right. I shouldn't have fallen asleep, anyway. What can I do for you?"

"Are you Miss Wilson?"

"Yes."

Steve grinned. "My name's Garrity, Miss Wilson. I saw your sign in town."

"Oh, yes. The gift shop."

"I was wondering if the building's still for rent."

She nodded. "Yes, it is. You think you might be interested in it, Mr. Garrity?" She had full, sensuous lips, Steve noticed, and even without lipstick they were very red. With just a little make-up, he decided, she would be a remarkably pretty girl.

"I think so," he said. "Of course, I've seen just the outside, but it seems to be pretty much what I had in mind."

"It's really a very nice location," she said, "Would you like to see it now, Mr. Garrity?"

"If it's convenient for you, yes."

"I'll be happy to show it to you. Is that your car out there at the curb?"

"Yes."

"I thought it must be. Leda—that's my niece—seems to have borrowed mine without bothering to tell me about it."

"I see."

"I'll have to do something about this hair," she said, moving around him to open the screen door. "Wouldn't you rather wait inside?"

"Thanks," Steve said as he followed her into the living room. "This is a nice place you've got here."

She smiled and motioned him to a seat on an old-fashioned davenport. "I'll just be a moment. Make yourself comfortable, Mr. Garrity."

Steve studied her as she left the room through a draped archway opposite the front door. She wasn't slim at all, he saw; not where it counted. She was a small girl with small bones and good legs, and the hips beneath the taut skirt were full and round. She would probably fool you in the front, too, he reflected: these small-boned girls were often bigger-busted than they looked.

He glanced about the living room, trying to remember how long it had been since he'd been in one like it. Not long enough, he decided; there was something about dark wallpaper and old-fashioned furniture that depressed him. It reminded him too vividly of the gloomy living room in which he had spent too many rainy days as a child. There were two overstuffed chairs, both with worn slip covers and small lumpy ottomans, a long library table with an empty vase sitting on a crocheted centerpiece, and a flowered rug worn thin. Against the wall beside the draped archway was an ancient upright piano with intricate carvings and scrollwork and time-yellowed keys.

Partly amused, partly curious, Steve walked over to the piano and let his left hand drift up the keyboard in a chromatic run. He was surprised to find that the piano was in perfect tune and less than half a note off concert pitch. The notes came rich and clean and the hammer action was as responsive as that of the piano in his apartment back in New York.

He worked up a beat in the bass and was just about to mix in a little froth in the treble when he noticed the picture in the easel frame at one end of the piano top. It was a tinted photograph of a little girl about four years old, sitting on a hassock and holding a striped rubber ball very tightly with both hands as if she were afraid it might get away from her. She was trying to smile but not quite making it, and her blue eyes seemed close to tears. There was a row of small white bows down the front of her short blue dress and a very large white bow atop the light brown waves of her hair.

Steve stopped playing and stood looking at the little girl.

"Hello, Leda," he said softly. "For a minute there I didn't recognize you."

Grinning to himself, he sat down on the bench and played a few bars of boogie, just to see whether the old upright would pick up a roar, the way most of them did. It didn't.

He walked back to the davenport and sat down again and crossed his legs. Outside, some children went by on roller skates, and from somewhere in the neighborhood a lawn mower measured the width of somebody's yard, paused, and started back the other way.

When Nancy Wilson came back into the room she had put on lipstick and changed to a white cotton dress and very high heels. Steve found himself staring at her in genuine appreciation.

"Sorry I was so long," she said, laughing. "This *hair!*"

"That's all right," Steve said, "Besides, I was interested in your piano."

"I heard you. Are you a professional?"

"Well ..."

She smiled. "I thought you must be. You're really quite good."

"I don't play boogie much," Steve said. "But it's a good way to see how much a piano's got in the bass." He nodded. "This one's really got it."

"I've always loved that old piano. I took lessons on it when I was a little girl."

"You still play?"

"Oh, no. Not for years. I keep it tuned for my niece."

"She's taking lessons, is she?"

"She was, up until this summer. But she seems to have lost interest."

"That's too bad."

"She's only fifteen, though. Maybe she'll take it up again. There's plenty of time."

The hell there is, Steve thought wryly. He opened the screen for her and they walked down to the car.

"This your home town, Miss Wilson?" he asked as he started the motor.

"Yes. I've lived here all my life."

"I envy you. It's a beautiful town."

"You like small towns, Mr. Garrity?"

"Call me Steve, why don't you? Yes, I like them very much."

"So do I. They have their shortcomings, I suppose, but all in all I wouldn't want to live anywhere else."

"I don't blame you," he said. "Me, I've lived most of my life in cities. New York mostly. I can really appreciate a place like this." He glanced at her from the corner of his eye. By God, she *was* full-busted; she couldn't have faked that much cleavage even if she'd fastened them together at the bottom with adhesive tape, the way the showgirls and models did.

"May I ask what you intend to do with the shop, Steve?" she said.

"Sure. I was thinking of opening a music store. You know, handle sheet music and records—maybe even a few record players and band instruments." He paused. "What's your opinion, Miss Wilson? Do you—"

"Nancy."

He smiled. "All right. Nancy.... Well, Nancy, what do you think of the idea?"

She twisted around in the seat, facing him, and drew one leg up beneath her. "I think it's a wonderful idea," she said, smoothing her skirt out carefully. "There'd be no place like it within miles of here."

"I like the location—just off the square, and all."

She nodded. "I think it would be ideal."

Of course you do, he thought. That's why you went broke in the gift-shop racket.

"May I ask you something else?" she said. "This really isn't any of my business, but——"

"That's all right. What is it?"

"Well, I'm just curious. You play the piano so well I wonder that you'd want to give it up—playing professionally, I mean."

Steve kept his eyes straight ahead. Here it comes, baby, he thought; you'd better duck. "It isn't a matter of wanting to, Nancy," he said quietly. "It's just a matter of age."

"Of age? Oh, really now, Steve. You must be joking."

"No," he said. "I'm serious. Jazz piano men hit their peak when they're in their early twenties, usually. They can stretch it out for six or eight years, sometimes a little longer. But after that it's pretty hard to keep up with the younger men, the ones just coming on. All at once you're working in somebody's pickup band, and mighty lucky to get it."

She seemed perplexed. "Why, you make yourself sound like an old man. Surely you can't mean that——"

"I'm thirty," Steve said. "And thirty isn't young, not in the music business. It's sort of like boxing or big-league baseball. I've been playing professionally since I was sixteen, Nancy. That's fourteen years. Your style dates, you see. You just don't have the drive any more."

She shook her head incredulously. "At thirty?"

"At thirty." He paused. "And besides, I'm getting just a little tired of it. I'd like to settle down and grow a few roots and—well, just be able to take a deep breath once in a while."

Which was filling a good crock full enough, he decided. It was time to change the key.

"Why'd you close up your gift shop, Nancy?" he asked. "Get tired of the headaches?"

"No, it wasn't that," she said. "I guess I'm just not much of a businesswoman, Steve. Everything I sold, the other stores sold cheaper. The dollar store and the five-and-ten. They could order an item by the gross, and get a big discount. I could only order it by the dozen. You wouldn't think a penny or so more would make so much difference to people, but it does."

"I know," Steve said.

"I suppose I should have held a going-out-of-business sale," she said. "But I didn't. I don't know, I'd hoped someone would take the shop over just as it was, stock and all."

Steve drove in silence for a while, trying to decide on a way to lead the conversation around to Leda without being too obvious about it. Actually, it would be better to wait for Nancy to cue him in, but it was beginning to look as if that might not happen.

"I just thought of something," he said. "You say your niece— What's her name?"

"Leda."

"Yes. Leda. Well if she's fifteen she must still be in high school, right?"

"Yes. She'll be a junior next year."

"Does she have a summer job somewhere?"

"No. Why?"

"Well, I was just thinking. A girl that age would know all the kids around here, and most of my customers for records and sheet music will be kids, so it just seemed to me that maybe she could be a big help in the store. She'd know just what the kids go for. And even if she could only work there a few weeks, until school started, it would give me a chance to get set." He paused. "You think she'd be interested?"

Nancy pursed her lips thoughtfully for a moment. "I just don't know." she said. "She's been acting very strange lately."

"Strange?"

"Well, perhaps that isn't just the right word. But for the last few weeks she's been almost like a different girl, somehow. Of course, a girl that age seems to change over-night, but ..." She shrugged helplessly. "She's been so moody and quiet lately. And she had an offer of a summer job only about two weeks ago. A very well-paying one, too. But she wouldn't take it. I just don't know what to tell you, Steve."

He forced himself to smile. "Girls that age don't know their own minds from one day to the next," he said. "Maybe after I meet her father and mother ..."

"Her mother's dead."

"Your sister?"

"Yes."

Steve shook his head sympathetically. "That's too bad, Nancy. I'm sorry to hear it." He was silent for a proper interval, and then said, "Well, I'll talk to her father, then. Maybe he can help me convince her." He threw it away and waited again, anxious to hear what Nancy might say about a man he knew was in the county jail, and hoping to find out why he was there. It was important. There was a damn good chance that the reason Noland was in jail had a connection with the reason the syndicate wanted his daughter murdered. Hell, it was more than a good chance; it was almost a certainty. And the more he knew about the setup, the better he could lay his plan, the safer he would be.

"That won't be possible," Nancy said. "He—he's away."

"Oh? Well, when he comes back, then."

"I'm afraid that may not be for some time," she said.

Steve nodded. "I see. He left her in your care, did he?"

"Yes. You turn right at the next corner."

Just like that. The freeze-out. So let it lie.

And change the key again.

"What'd you do, Nancy?" he said. "I mean, before you opened the gift shop?"

"I taught school," she said. "Kindergarten and first grade."

"I don't believe it."

She smiled. "If that's a compliment, thank you."

"You're welcome."

She glanced out the window. "We're almost there, Steve. Perhaps you'd better look for a parking space."

Steve protracted his inspection of the building just long enough to be convincing, and then walked back to where Nancy stood waiting near the door.

"It's exactly right, Nancy," he said. "All I'd need are a couple of record booths and a few extra shelves, and I'll be in business."

"I'm so glad you like it," she said. "Would you say that two hundred a month would be about right?"

"That'll be fine," he said. "Suppose I give you a deposit now, and then pay the balance on the first."

She nodded. "I'll write you a receipt when we get back to the house." She glanced about the shop, smiling a little sadly. "And I wish you all the luck in the world, Steve; I really do."

Standing so close to her like this, he could smell the fragrance of her hair, and another, more subtle fragrance that was neither soap nor perfume but something else, some natural fragrance of her own.

"I'm sure you do, Nancy," he said warmly. "Thanks very much."

Outside, Steve opened the car door for her and

then walked around the hood to get behind the wheel.

It was then that he saw the man on the opposite sidewalk. He glanced at him, opened the door, then turned his head quickly to glance at him again.

The man was somewhere in his middle thirties, a tall blond man with a powerful-looking, wedge-shaped body and a square, sunburned face with small, almost effeminate features. But it was his eyes that had made Steve turn to look at him again. They were very pale eyes, slightly hooded at the outer corners, and they were fixed on Steve with as much naked hatred as Steve had ever seen.

Steve shrugged and got behind the wheel. "Who's your friend, Nancy?" he asked as he closed the door. "That character over there on the far curb."

Nancy lowered her head to look through Steve's window, then straightened quickly and looked away. "No one," she said. "Don't think anything about him."

"He doesn't seem to think much of me, either," Steve said. "What goes? He a boy friend of yours?"

"No, of course not," she said, frowning. "Please, Steve. Start the car."

He drove half a block, then turned to smile at her. "Who is that guy, Nancy? That's the damnedest look I ever got from anybody."

Nancy smoothed her skirt down over her knees. She was still frowning, still not looking at him. "Don't let him worry you, Steve."

"He doesn't worry me one bit," Steve said, studying her face. "Should he?"

"Of course not. It's just— Well, he just isn't all there."

"There's plenty of him there," Steve said. "You could make two average-sized guys out of him and still have enough—"

"He stares at all strangers that way," Nancy said.

"For a guy with a habit like that, he's lived a long

time."

Nancy smiled thinly. "The only thing you can do about him is ignore him."

"He'd make that pretty tough to do."

"Turn at the next corner," she said. "That's Elm. You can follow Elm straight on out to High Street."

"All right," Steve said. "One character seen and forgotten, okay?"

Nancy nodded but said nothing, and she was withdrawn and untalkative during the drive back to her house. Steve tried several times to reach her, but finally he sensed that this was futile, and he gave up and limited himself to an occasional observation on the houses and people they passed in the car. He was beginning to feel a vague unease. The look in the blond man's eyes hadn't been just hate, but a jealous hate. He'd seen too much jealous hate not to recognize it, and recognize it instantly. And a man with that kind of hate could be dangerous, he knew; a man like that could get in the way at just the wrong time and foul things up to hell and gone. Anyone who could work up so much hate so quickly, and who could affect Nancy Wilson so profoundly, was a man to watch. And a man who would, undoubtedly, be watching *him*.

CHAPTER FIVE

There was a very old Chevrolet coupe parked directly in front of Nancy's house, and Steve drew to a stop behind it.

"Well," Nancy said. "I see that Leda finally brought my car back." She smiled, just a little too brightly, and Steve sensed that she was trying desperately to wrench her thoughts away from wherever they had been during the ride back from the gift shop.

Steve grinned. "I'm glad she didn't decide to abscond with it," he said. "But isn't fifteen pretty young to be driving a car, Nancy?"

"Not around here. She has her father's written permission on file downtown, and that's all it takes." She laughed. "They wouldn't think very much of that in New York, would they?"

"No."

"She's really a very good little driver. You'd be surprised."

He got out, opened the door on Nancy's side, and followed her up to the porch. A girl could have an accident in a car, he reflected; it happened all the time. The trick was to make it happen on purpose.

As they entered the living room, Nancy smiled at the girl sitting on the arm of one of the easy chairs, and then turned to Steve.

"Steve," she said, "this is my niece, Leda. Leda, this is Mr. Garrity."

The picture Licardi had shown him back in New York hadn't told the whole story, Steve saw. It had told him that Leda was beautiful, but it hadn't conveyed the young-girl freshness of her skin, or the light brown hair that had just a tinge of red in it where a ray of sunlight struck it, or the blue eyes that were so dark that at first they seemed almost purple. And even her loose plaid shirt and worn blue jeans only served to enhance the full-blown curves beneath them.

Steve moistened his lips. "Hello, Leda," he said. "How are you?"

She smiled at him. "Just fine, thanks," she said, and then looked at Nancy. "I hope you didn't mind my using the Chevy. I would have asked you, but you were asleep and I didn't want to wake you."

"Don't give it another thought," Nancy said fondly. "I'm becoming used to your ways in spite of myself."

"I won't do it again," Leda said. "That's a promise."

"Take it any time you like," Nancy said. "And please sit down, Steve. I'll make out your receipt for the deposit, and we can draw up a lease on the first."

Steve sat down on the davenport and reached for a cigarette. "Make it out for fifty dollars," he said. "That all right with you, Nancy?"

"Yes, of course."

"Deposit on what?" Leda said.

"Mr. Garrity's renting the shop, dear," Nancy said. "He's going to open a music store."

"Oh, really?" Leda said. "You mean with booths where people can play records and all?"

"Yep," Steve said, grinning. "Booths and all. The works."

Nancy smiled and walked to the draped archway that led to the rear of the house. "That should give you two something in common," she said. "Back in a minute, Steve."

Steve lit his cigarette and shook out the match slowly, trying to decide just how to handle this. Before he could plan Leda's accident, he would first have to know where and when such an accident might logically take place. He'd have to know her habits—what she did and where she went, and who her friends were, and everything else. Then, and only then, could he decide on the way she was to die.

But pump her gently, he reminded himself. Crowd the tempo a little too much and you'll cut your own throat.

"Well, Leda," he said, "what do you think of it?"

"You mean, about your starting a music store?"

"Yes. Nancy tells me there's none within several miles of here."

She nodded. "That's right. I'd think you ought to do very well."

"I was wondering whether you might not like to help me out."

"How?"

"Well, you know all the kids around here, and—"

"Kids?"

He grinned. "I beg your pardon. I meant to say 'younger people,' of course. People your own age. They'll be my biggest customers, and I thought it would be a big help to me if you could work in the shop for a week or so, until school started."

She shook her head. "I'm really not interested in a job, Mr. Garrity."

"The pay would be pretty good, Leda. How's forty a week sound to you?"

"For around here, it sounds fabulous. But I'm not interested, Mr. Garrity. Really."

"Not even for a week or so?"

She shook her head. "No. But there are a lot of girls who would be. Almost any of them would. You won't have any trouble at all."

"Well, I just don't know," Steve said doubtfully. "Not many girls have had your experience, Leda."

"You must mean my piano lessons." She smiled. "I'm afraid Nancy's been bragging about me again."

"Everything helps, of course," Steve said. "But I was thinking more about your experience with the high-school band. I'm planning to stock band instruments too, you know."

She slid down into the bottom of her chair, leaving her legs dangling over the arm. "But I don't play in the band, Mr. Garrity. I—"

"No, but you're a drum majorette, and that amounts to the same thing. You know all the boys and girls in the band, and with school about to open again, a lot of them will be buying new trumpets and trombones and whatever." He paused. "You see what I mean, Leda? If I had a girl who knew all these kids, and their parents too, probably—well, that wouldn't do my business any harm, now would it?"

"No," she said quietly, "I don't suppose it would."

I put it up to her too bluntly, Steve thought. I made it sound like I wanted her to help me con the damn kids out of their dough or something.

"Don't misunderstand me, Leda," he said. "It's just that I'm new here, and I'll need someone to introduce me to the people I hope to do business with. I certainly didn't mean that I would expect you to—"

"I didn't misunderstand you, Mr. Garrity," she said. "But I'm simply not interested."

"I see," Steve said. "Well, maybe you'll change your mind. If you do, let me know."

Before he could think of another gambit, Nancy Wilson came back into the room. Steve started to get up, but she gestured for him to keep his seat.

"Watch the ink," she said, handing him a receipt form. "I think it's still a little wet."

Steve took out his wallet, gave Nancy one of the fifty-dollar bills, and then folded the receipt without looking at it and tucked it into his wallet.

From somewhere back in the house a phone had begun to ring.

"I forgot to tell you," Leda said. "There was a call for you, Nancy. Just before you came in."

"Who was it?" Nancy said.

"Del," Leda said. "He said he'd call back. Sorry I forgot."

Nancy frowned and left the room again.

Was Del the blond man who'd stared at them from the curb? Steve wondered. Or might it be still another of Nancy's men friends, still another man for Steve to make jealous and watchful? And the hell of it was, there might be more. Just how far could he stretch things out before one of them stepped in and knocked over the apple cart?

That's right, he told himself angrily. You haven't got enough troubles already, so go ahead and invent a few. Cross all the bridges before you get to them, like a fool.

"... guess you didn't hear me," Leda was saying.

He looked at her sharply, then shook his head. "I'm sorry," he said. "I must have been woolgathering."

She smiled. "I do that myself sometimes. I was asking you where you were from."

"New York," he said. "At least, I call that my home town."

"Won't Garrensville be a little slow for you?"

"I don't think so," he said. "But if it does, I can always go back for a weekend."

For some moments now, Steve had been able to hear Nancy's voice as she talked on the phone, but he had not been able to make out what she was saying. But suddenly her voice rose in anger and he heard her say, "No, Del!... No. Absolutely not!" And then, just as abruptly, her voice fell again and he could make out nothing.

This Del must be a sad case, he reflected. Probably calling to third-degree her about the man he'd seen her with at the gift shop, and probably sweating her out over something that even an idiot should have made for nothing more than a business talk between a property owner and a prospective tenant. And if he could get so steamed up over anything as innocent as that, what would he be like when he really got rolling?

"We have some cold beer in the icebox, Mr. Garrity," Leda said. "Would you like me to bring you a bottle?"

"Thanks," Steve said. "I could use one."

Leda got up and had almost reached the draped archway when Nancy came through it from the other direction.

"Steve," she said, "something's come up. I'm afraid we'll have to postpone our talk till another time." Her gray eyes were angry and there was a thin white line above the deep bow of her upper lip. "I—

I'm terribly sorry, Steve."

All right, Steve thought as he got to his feet; you don't have to cue me with a brick wall. "There're some things I should take care of this afternoon, anyhow," he said, smiling pleasantly. "And there's no rush at all, so far as our business is concerned, Nancy. Perhaps we can talk about it again tomorrow."

"Yes, that'll be fine," Nancy said. "Call me whenever you like."

Steve hesitated a moment, then said good-by to both Nancy and Leda and stepped out onto the porch. When he was halfway down the walk, he glanced back over his shoulder. Leda's small, perfect body was framed in the shaded doorway like a silhouette. She was standing with one hand to her throat, smiling at him; but there was something strange about her smile, something almost hard.

Steve waved to her and walked down to his car. It was difficult to keep the frustration and anger from his face as he got into the car and drove off, and he dropped the mask as soon as he knew he was out of sight of the house.

What had begun so beautifully had ended abruptly and fruitlessly. He'd learned nothing at all about Leda Noland except that she was unlike any other fifteen-year-old girl he had ever known. He'd known a great many girls Leda's age, all the way from the switchblade-carrying members of girl gangs to the polished, sophisticated products of Sutton Place and Park Avenue; but he'd never known a Leda, or anyone even remotely like her.

He swore softly, careening the car around the corner so viciously that he narrowly missed colliding with a pickup truck coming in the opposite direction.

All the old questions were still there. He still didn't know one thing about Leda; he still didn't know why her father was in the county jail; he still didn't know how he was going to kill her; he still didn't know why the syndicate wanted her dead.

He still didn't know *anything*.

Then, suddenly, he remembered the terror of that rainy night in Missouri, and his hands clutched the steering wheel so tightly that his knuckles ached.

CHAPTER SIX

By the time Steve reached the square and parked the car, it was almost five o'clock. He remained in the car for several minutes while he watched the flow of pedestrians on the sidewalk; then he got out, located a haberdashery, and bought two short-sleeved sport shirts. So far, he had not seen even one other man in a tie and jacket, and he had begun to feel conspicuous.

I've got to relax and be one of the folks, he thought as he walked back to his hotel. I've got to act like a man who intends to set himself up in business here.

It wasn't going to be easy, he knew. His cover story needed nailing down; just making a deposit on Nancy Wilson's store building wasn't enough. He didn't intend to let go of any more of Licardi's fifty-dollar bills than he had to, but still he had to make things look the way they should. All he had to do was raise just one question in just one person's mind, and he'd had it.

He entered the lobby of the hotel, crossed to the desk, and stood smiling at Mrs. Conklin. The hillbilly music still wailed from the radio at her elbow and the overhead fan still labored loudly without doing anything to the air.

"Two-o-six, please," he said.

Mrs. Conklin twisted her enormous body a few inches to the left, reached into the mail rack without looking at it, and dropped Steve's key on the desk.

You really ought to do something about that fat, Steve thought. They don't make caskets your size.

One of these days you're going to drop dead, and they'll have to pry you out of there and haul you away in a rather large truck.

"I was wondering if I could leave some money in your safe," he said.

She frowned at him. "How much?"

"Only a couple of hundred," Steve said. "I meant to open a bank account this afternoon, but I got back a little too late."

"Don't apologize," she said. "It's part of the service." She reached beneath the desk and handed Steve a small brown envelope. "Put it in there, and then write the amount and your name on the flap and seal it up yourself."

When Steve returned the envelope to her, she pushed it to one side and stood drumming her fingertips on the desktop. "Anything else you wanted?"

Steve picked up his key. "Not unless you happen to know where I could find a good carpenter," he said. "I'm going to open a music store here, Mrs. Conklin. I'll be needing some shelves and booths and so on." He paused thoughtfully. "And a paint job too, I think."

"You sure will," she said. "That place has needed painting for a long time."

He looked at her blankly.

"You're taking Nancy Wilson's place, aren't you?" she said.

"Yes, but—"

"Somebody mentioned they saw her showing it to you," she said. "Things like that get around."

"I see."

"And I can tell you one thing right now," she said happily. "You'll go broke. There's no money in this town, Mr. Garrity. Never has been—at least, not since they built the new highway."

"Still—"

"Don't tell me. I know what I'm talking about."

She shrugged. "But that's your lookout, not mine. If it's a carpenter you want, you might try Ed Runyons, over at the funeral parlor. He's a little slow, but once he does a job it's done right."

"Thanks," Steve said. "I'll look him up first thing in the morning."

"You better. That's just about the only time you're apt to find him sober."

Steve nodded and turned to buy a package of cigarettes from the vending machine behind him. "I give you two months," Mrs. Conklin said. "Three, at the outside."

He stripped the cellophane from the package, lit a cigarette, and dropped the cellophane and the burned match into a cuspidor near the desk. "You don't sound very encouraging," he said.

"Why should I kid you?" She turned the radio down a little lower and leaned her forearms on the desk. "What'd you think of Nancy Wilson?"

He watched the way the flabby flesh of Mrs. Conklin's ponderous arms spread out on the desktop. "A lovely girl," he said. "We got along fine."

"You meet her niece? Leda?"

"Yes. She was there when I took Miss Wilson home."

"Too bad about her, isn't it?"

"You mean Leda? I don't think I know what you—"

"Yes. Leda. Her father being an embezzler and all. Too bad."

Steve shook his head. "I hadn't heard anything about it, Mrs. Conklin," he said.

"They've got him over to the county jail. That's why Leda's staying with Nancy. And it's a good thing she is, too. A real pretty one like that needs looking after even more than most of them."

"I suppose so," Steve said.

"You saw her, didn't you? Then you know what

I mean. You don't see a girl like that every time you turn around."

"I'm sorry to hear about her father," Steve said carefully. "An embezzler, you say?" He shook his head. "That's a terrible thing to happen."

"Don't seem to bother her too much, though, does it?"

"Well ... now that you mention it, Mrs. Conklin, I—"

"Don't bother her one bit. Here her father's been what you might call a respected member of the community for—let's see—almost twenty years now, and all of a sudden he turns into a criminal. Funny how men'll do, isn't it?"

Steve nodded. "I guess you just never know about people," he said.

"You can say that again." She shook her head. "Odd, isn't it?"

"What's that, Mrs. Conklin?"

"Why, that Leda can hold her head up around here. She does, though. She comes twitching down the street just the same as before. The way that girl acts, you'd think her father'd gone off to Congress, instead of to jail." She picked up Steve's envelope and turned to open the safe on the floor beneath the mail rack. "Well, you go see Ed Runyons tomorrow morning. Just keep him off the bottle long enough and he'll do a good job for you."

"Thanks for the tip," Steve said. "I'll keep an eye on him." He picked up his key, climbed the stairs to the second floor, and let himself into his room.

So Leda's old man had been thrown in jail for embezzlement, he reflected. At least he'd learned that much, if nothing else. But so what? What could there be about a small-town embezzler that would interest the syndicate? There had to be something, sure—but what? The syndicate certainly wouldn't order the execution of a teen-aged girl just because her father had got caught tapping the till, even if the till happened to belong to the syndicate itself.

What was it that Licardi had said? "All you got to worry about is seeing that she don't get any older."

Sure, Steve thought bitterly; that's the only worry I've got in the world.

He stayed in his room only long enough to throw some cold water on his face and change to one of the sport shirts he had bought at the haberdashery. Then he went back downstairs, got into the Ford, and began to case Garrensville as systematically and thoroughly as possible.

He drove along all four sides of the square three times, and along all the surrounding side streets at least twice, but he didn't find what he was looking for. He could find no place at all where an accident could be expected to happen, or even a place where one could be arranged to happen. There were no natural hazards, nothing he could rig so that it would become a hazard. He was forced to think again of the two obvious possibilities that had occurred to him at once, and which he had, almost as quickly, discarded as too risky.

First, Leda could fall down a flight of stairs and die of a broken neck. Second, she could become the victim of a hit-and-run driver.

In the case of a fall, he would need fantastic luck. He'd have to approach Leda, unseen by either Leda or anyone else, and break her neck before she could cry out. Then, after he'd started her body on its way down the stairs, he'd have to get away before the sound of her fall drew attention and he was seen. For a man of his size and muscular development, breaking a small girl's neck would be no problem at all; but approaching her, killing her, and getting away without being seen by some unexpected witness—that was something else again.

And to arrange for Leda to be the victim of a hit-

and-run driver would require even more luck than to arrange for her death by a fall. It would mean not only that he would have to steal a car for the purpose, but that he would also have to maneuver Leda into being at a specific place at a specific time. Further, to insure her not crying out, he would have to kill her outright the first time he struck her. And even if his luck held out that far, it would be next to impossible to steal a car, drive it to the spot where Leda would be, remain in it while he waited for her, and then make his getaway—all without being seen by someone who could later identify him.

No, Steve thought. Both ways were out. One was as dangerous as the other. They were barely even possibilities; they were merely desperation measures, to be thought about again only if everything else failed. A hit—any hit at all—was risky enough, even when you kept it simple and figured all the angles.

But how did you figure angles when there were no angles to figure?

You played it by ear.

Sure.

But how?

It always came back to that: How?

This was the dinner hour, and the streets around the square were almost deserted. Steve parked near the same restaurant where he had had lunch, and went inside.

He wasn't hungry, and he found himself annoyed by the covert glances the other diners cast his way, but he forced himself to eat. He'd learned from experience that a man of his size couldn't miss too many meals without finding cause to regret it.

The same waitress who had served him his lunch also served him his dinner. She was a very thin, very large-boned girl with slightly protuberant eyes and a jaw like a clenched fist.

"That's funny," she said as she brought his

check. "You have coffee and brandy with your lunch, but you don't have it with your dinner."

"That's funny?" Steve said.

She gave him a wet smile with a lot of teeth in it. "I mean, it seems to me it should be the other way around."

He forced a grin. "You're right," he said. "I guess I got it a little backward." If I could once get into that house on High Street, when Leda was home and Nancy wasn't, and if I could get in and out again without being spotted by one of the neighbors ...

"We serve up to midnight," the waitress said. "That's when I get off, at midnight."

"Maybe I might drop back about that time," Steve said. "You think that would be a good idea?" I could break her neck, and strip her, and put her in the bathtub. All I'd have to do is bang her head against the rim of the tub and turn the shower on, and it'd look like she slipped and fell and ...

"It might," the waitress said. "It just might be a pretty good idea, at that." She leaned her thin thigh against the edge of Steve's table, rubbing against it, an inch forward, an inch back.

"I hope I can get away by then," Steve said. "I wouldn't want you to think I'd stood you up." How many accidents happened in bathrooms? He'd read the statistics once; they'd been fantastic. People slipped in showers and bathtubs every day, killed themselves that way all the time....

"No later than eleven-forty-five, though," the waitress said, leaning down to collect the dirty dishes. "Sometimes it slows up and the boss lets me off a little early." She tucked her dollar tip into the pocket of her apron, glanced meaningfully at the clock over the service bar, and moved away toward the kitchen.

Steve left the restaurant and paused just outside the door to light a cigarette. There were even fewer people abroad now than there had been when he had gone inside. He inhaled deeply on his cigarette, looked at the Indian warrior in the middle of the square, and shook his head slowly.

You'd better get that arrow out in a hurry, brother, he said to himself. It's later than you think.

Chapter Seven

Steve walked halfway around the almost completely deserted square, and then, feeling suddenly depressed, he turned in at a small bar and ordered a beer. He didn't particularly want the beer, but he felt the need of other people around him and the beer would be something to stall with until his depression passed.

There was something about this time of evening, midway between sunset and darkness, that always made him feel as if the world were dying about him. In New York he almost never spent these hours on the street; when they came, he went into dim saloons where the fading daylight made no difference in the soft neon sheen of the bottles behind the bar and the twilight passed imperceptibly into night. Even in his apartment he always drew the drapes across the windows to hide the gradual death of the world outside. When he had been younger, the twilight hours had induced something close to panic; and even now, at thirty, his near panic was still there, consciously repressed and controlled, but seeping up through the levels of his awareness to evoke the feeling of depression, of utter aloneness.

He glanced about him. It was a workingman's bar, a long, narrow room with rickety booths and bleak gray walls. Above the strident pounding of guitar music from the jukebox were the overloud, desperately happy voices of men who were trying to forget the frustration of the jobs they had just left, or of the homes they had to go to, or both.

Steve smiled wryly, making wet interlocking circles with the bottom of his glass. The bar reminded him of other bars along Madison Avenue and around Grand Central Station, where other kinds of workingmen, from television and advertising, gathered for a few fast drinks between their jobs and the next commuters' train. The clothing and the talk and the drinks were different, but the need was the same.

Poor damn squares, he thought. What a hell of a way to live.

He sipped at his beer, trying to think of nothing. Another hour; then it would be dark enough and he could go outside.

But night came more abruptly here than it did in New York. Half an hour later the street lights came on, and when Steve glanced through the plate-glass window he saw that it was dark. He put a tip on the bar and went outside.

The streets were beginning to come to life again. There were cars and pickup trucks and station wagons in most of the diagonal parking spaces along the curbs, and on the corners there were clusters of younger men watching the girls who paraded past them in twos and threes. The young couples on the green had given way to older couples with children, but the benches once again were lined with old men, most of them now wearing sweaters or vests and hats of one kind or another.

Steve walked to the Ford and got in and drove out of town. He felt the need of movement, of the feeling of control and power that always came with the operation of an automobile; and he wanted to explore the countryside around the town. There wasn't too much he could see at night, but still there might be some place where he could rig Leda's accident. An abandoned quarry where she might fall. A drop-off near a road where she might be sideswiped by another car. Anything. And even if he found no

natural props to help him plan her death, he wanted
to know the roads around Garrensville as well as he
knew the streets around his apartment back in New
York. There might be time when his knowledge of
them could mean the difference between life and
death.

Two hours later, he started back to town. He had
driven over asphalt and macadam and gravel and tar
and rutted dirt, and although he now knew the roads
around Garrensville as well as he could reasonably
expect to know them, he had found nothing whatever
that he could utilize in a planned accident.

When he reached the square, he found that all the
parking spaces near the hotel had been taken, and he
drove along slowly, looking for a place to leave the
car.

He found one not far from the entrance of the
movie house, and he sat there, smoking thoughtfully,
trying to decide on his next move. He glanced at his
watch. It was almost ten o'clock—just a little too late
to call Nancy Wilson. And besides, she had chased
him off immediately after she'd got that call from Del,
which could only mean that Del had been on his way
over to see her and would, in all probability, still be
with her. But whether he was with her or not, this
was a little too soon for another session with her. A
visit at this time of night would have to be justified,
and if he failed to justify it—which would be difficult—he might arouse suspicion. There was a limit to
how much he could pump her about Leda without
raising a question in her mind; and so far as pumping
Leda herself was concerned, he had a strong feeling
that he'd get no more than he had this afternoon:
nothing. All in all, he decided, the time just wasn't
right. It would be much better, and safer, to postpone
his next attempt until tomorrow.

He sat watching the people entering and leaving
the movie house for a few minutes, trying to think of

every conceivable kind of accident a girl like Leda might have, and then he sat bolt upright and strained his eyes along the sidewalk.

There were two teen-aged girls approaching the movie house, and he had been right: One of the girls was Leda. Steve sank down in the seat, cursing the light from the marquee that slanted onto his face through the windshield.

The two girls paused in front of the placard just outside the entrance, studying it. The other girl was an ash blonde, about the same size as Leda but a little plumper and not pretty at all. Leda still wore the same plaid shirt and blue jeans she had had on when Steve met her; the blonde girl wore a white blouse and a flowered dirndl skirt. They seemed to be having some trouble making up their minds whether or not they wanted to see the movie. Once they started toward the ticket window, and then paused, talked for a moment, and walked back to look at the stills on the placard again.

Well, Steve thought, what's the difference? She's with someone, isn't she? And even if she weren't, what could you do to her in a movie house?

But maybe she would walk home alone. And if she did, then what? He couldn't do a thing. Kill her, yes—in any of a dozen different ways—but not so that it would look like an accident.

Leda and the other girl were attracting attention, Steve saw; or rather, Leda was attracting it. The boys and younger men in her vicinity hadn't moved or spoken since she came within sight. They were all looking at her as if they were in awe of her—as if they had somehow convinced themselves that a girl this pretty couldn't be quite real. There were none of the suggestive comments they had made about the other young girls who had passed them, none of the smirking looks with which they had appraised them.

Licardi hadn't overstated it, Steve reflected. Leda

Noland would be the center of attention always, no matter where she happened to be or what she happened to be doing. Even in the plaid shirt and blue jeans, even standing in the harsh white light of the marquee with her face only partly made up and her brown hair in a pony tail, she was easily one of the most beautiful girls Steve had ever seen. And if she was that to him, a man who had been around professional beauties half his life, what must she be like for people in a small, cut-off town like Garrensville?

Leda seemed not to notice the awe, the near reverence paid her by the silent watchers about her. She chatted for a moment with the other girl, then turned away from the placard, locked her arm in the other girl's, and started back up the sidewalk in the direction from which she had come. A few steps farther on she and the other girl paused, apparently to talk to someone in a car parked at the curb.

Steve sat up straight again. Leda and the blonde girl were talking to two boys in a topless jalopy. Then both girls got in, Leda in the front seat and her friend in the back, and the jalopy pulled away. The boys and men on the sidewalk still hadn't moved or spoken, and other young girls strolled past them completely unnoticed.

Steve watched the jalopy draw away from the curb; and then, on impulse, he started his own car and followed it. The chances of being able to do anything to Leda while she remained with the others were hardly better than they would have been in the movie house, but following the jalopy was at least something to do, something to occupy him physically and mentally. And even though he couldn't get to Leda tonight, it was possible that following her would tell him a little more about her. And if she and the others parked somewhere—a lover's lane of some kind, for instance—and split up, he just might be able to work something out. He couldn't foresee any way to rig an accident, but that didn't mean that a way wouldn't present itself. It was better to follow her and hope than to sit around somewhere and do nothing at all.

He kept half a block behind the jalopy until it was out in the open countryside, and then let the distance increase slowly to half a mile. He had no fear of losing it, even at a greater distance than that; with no top and all the useless accessories on it, it was too easily identifiable. There was a long radio antenna projecting from each side of the windshield, a spotlight mounted high up on the driver's side, a chromium trunk rack, and wide rubber mud guards set with dozens of tiny red glass reflectors.

Steve fell back even more, allowing two other cars to pass and get between him and the jalopy. It was safer this way. If the kids should notice that anyone was following them, they probably wouldn't be able to see the Ford at all.

Four miles farther on the jalopy slowed, waited for the two intervening cars to pass it, and then swerved left into a bisecting road and picked up speed again.

The new road was well surfaced, but much narrower and more winding than the first had been. Steve kept his speed down until the jalopy's taillights were almost out of sight; and then, suddenly, there was nothing ahead of him at all. He drove a hundred yards farther, thinking the jalopy might have rounded a sharp curve, but the winding ribbon of the road stretched ahead of him for at least a mile, and his was the only car on it.

He hesitated. If the jalopy had pulled off the road, its occupants would see him go past. On the other hand, if he turned around and went back, he might call more attention to himself than if he went straight ahead. His indecision lasted only a moment, and then he speeded up and drove ahead, keeping a sharp lookout for a car parked at either side of the road.

Twenty yards ahead, he saw a faint red glow through the foliage of the trees and knew that it must be the red reflectors on the jalopy's mud guards.

There was nothing to do but go on, he knew; the slightest increase or decrease in speed would attract attention to his car, and parking anywhere nearby was out of the question.

He drove a full mile, then turned the car around and drove back. Above the place where the jalopy was parked he saw four small figures outlined against the sky at the top of a rise. His headlights bathed them for only a few seconds, but it was long enough for him to see them start down the other side.

It would be dangerous to follow them, he knew, and yet the temptation to do so was almost irresistible. The feeling of urgency was hammering at him again; he felt compelled to do something, anything, so long as there was any chance at all of killing Leda, or even a chance of learning more about her.

He drove all the way to the intersection and then parked on the shoulder for several minutes while he tried to argue himself out of the idea. But it was no good. This was something he felt he had to do, dangerous or not. He made a U turn and started back, driving even more slowly this time, looking for a place to hide the Ford.

He found one at last, not too far from the jalopy and well hidden from the road by trees and bushes. When he had driven into the trees as far as he could go, he got out and walked back to the road to see whether the Ford could be spotted from there. Then, satisfied it could not, he began to climb the rise.

This was the most risky part of all. If the kids should come back and see him here, he'd be through before he started. He climbed rapidly, thankful for the moonlight that made his way easier, but knowing what it would mean if Leda and her friends should return before he reached the top.

A few feet from the top he paused, motionless, listening intently. There was no sound. He raised his head slowly and looked down the other side. The ground fell away steeply toward a grove of tall trees, and through the trees he could see the sparkle of moonlight on water. Between Steve and the grove there were no trees at all, nothing to use as a cover on the way down, and the moon was very bright. But there were clouds in the sky, and he waited impatiently until one of them passed across the moon. Then he half ran down the slope to the grove and threaded his way through the trees to the edge of the water.

At first he thought he had come out on the bank of a stream, but when his eyes became more accustomed to the dark he saw that it was a small lake with a tiny island in the middle of it. There were trees on the island, and as he searched it with his eyes he saw something white arc out and up and then hang suspended in the air for an instant before it dropped straight down into the water.

So that's what they're up to, he thought. They've tied a rope to a tree limb and they're swinging out over the water as far as they can before they let go.

It was exactly the kind of thing he had been looking for—a place where Leda could have a fatal accident. But not while she was with three other people, and probably never; the chances of her coming here alone were too remote.

Another white figure swung out on the rope, hovered in the air a moment, and dropped. It was a girl, and she was nude.

Steve listened to the splash of her body as it met the water. It had been the other girl, the blonde. That much had been obvious, even with the moon still behind the cloud. She had been built like an adolescent, not like Leda Noland.

Then Leda swung out on the rope, and Steve sucked in his breath. The moon had come from behind the cloud just before she reached the top of her swing, and for a long moment her naked body seemed to be superimposed on the dark backdrop of the night behind her, the perfection of breasts and hips and legs silvered softly by the moonlight.

Steve moved a little nearer the edge of the water, then drew back suddenly as he heard a splashing sound within a few yards of him and realized that someone was swimming directly toward him. He had been crouching among the bushes; now he dropped to his stomach and flattened himself against the ground.

The swimmer came by the spot where Steve lay, but he was using a crawl stroke and not looking at the bank at all. A few yards behind him came the blonde girl, swimming on her back, moving through the water so silently that if Steve hadn't seen her he wouldn't have known she was there.

The boy who had come past was probably the same one Steve had seen swing out on the rope; and as no one had swung out on it for several minutes, the other boy in Leda's group must have dropped into the water before Steve arrived at the edge of the lake. And now they were coming past him, swimming in the same order in which they had dropped into the water. This, then, must be something like the children's game of follow-the-leader, with a swing on the rope, a circuit of the small island, another swing on the rope, and so on. And Leda had dropped into the water last, following the blonde girl, which meant that she would be swimming past him at almost any moment now.

He looked both ways along the bank. A few yards to his right was a large rock, almost a miniature island itself, about six feet from the bank. The blonde girl had just reached it, and to Steve's surprise, rather than swimming to the far side of it, she swam be-

tween it and the bank. Then he saw why. Between the
large rock and the island was a row of smaller, jagged
rocks that formed a sort of natural bridge, and
through which swimming would have been impossible.

He glanced in the other direction. He could see
Leda now, swimming on her back, just as the blonde
girl had done.

It's an absolute gift, he thought. I'll never have a
better chance. Hell, they just don't make them any
better.

Keeping well back in the trees and willows, he
hurried to a spot on the bank just opposite the big
rock and stripped himself to the skin, glancing in Leda's direction every few moments to make sure she
wasn't getting too close to the rock.

Then, naked, he crawled to the edge of the water
and glanced up at the moon. There was a large cloud
near the moon, but not near enough; it wouldn't cover it in time to do him any good. He couldn't risk
Leda's seeing him, even though she was swimming on
her back and it wasn't likely she'd look around. He
crawled forward into the water and swam beneath it
until his outstretched fingertips touched the side of
the rock. Then, still beneath the water, he worked his
way around the rock until he knew he had placed it
between himself and Leda.

But there was still the blonde girl to worry about,
and he raised his face to the surface very slowly, his
head thrown back so that only his nose and eyes
would be visible above the water.

The blonde girl was rounding the far end of the
island, still swimming on her back, and Steve had
only a fleeting glimpse of white as she scissored her
legs once more and disappeared completely.

He turned and pressed his body close to the rock,
listening to the tiny rhythmic splashes of Leda's back-
stroke. The water here was surprisingly deep for a

point so close to the bank, and when he spread his feet on the bottom and stood erect it came up almost to his chin. It was warm, still water, much warmer than the night air on his face and the cool slimy surface of the rock against his thigh and shoulder.

He stood there, breathing silently through his mouth, smiling a little as he listened to Leda approaching the narrow opening between the rock and the bank. He knew just how it would be; in his mind, it was already an accomplished act. And it would be the foolproof, accidental death the syndicate demanded.

Drowning was a silent death. He remembered when he was nine, and how it had been with Bobby Martin. They had taken the free swimming lessons at one of the public pools that summer, and he and Bobby had been "water buddies." The idea was that water buddies were responsible for each other, and whenever the instructor blew his whistle—as he did frequently—the pairs of water buddies were supposed to clasp hands and raise them, so that the instructor could see at a glance whether anyone was missing.

It had happened during the third lesson, when he and Bobby had been at the shallow end of the pool, practicing flutter kicks. The instructor had blown his whistle and Steve had knuckled the water from his eyes and turned toward the place where Bobby should have been.

Bobby had been there, but he was on the bottom, and he was dead. In less than two minutes, a boy had drowned almost within touching distance of a dozen other boys; and he had died so silently that not one of the other boys had even known he was in trouble.

Death by drowning was a silent death—and, accomplished properly, would leave no telltale marks on either Steve or his victim.

Steve pressed his hard body against the rock and strained his ears. She could be no more than a dozen feet away, he judged; he could even hear the sound of her breathing now.

It would be easy. When Leda began to swim past the rock, he would submerge, crawl to the middle of the passage between the rock and the bank, and wait for her on the bottom. When she passed overhead, he would jerk her body beneath the surface so quickly that she would have no chance to cry out. Then, pinioning her arms to her sides with his left arm and clamping her legs between his own, he would strike her sharply in the stomach with his right fist. Reflex action would suck water into her nose and mouth almost instantly; and with her arms and legs held securely, she would be unable to struggle at all. She would drown, and drown quickly, and she would do it without ever having uttered a sound. And later, when they found her, they would see only the unmarked body of a girl who had met her death as silently and as accidentally as Bobby Martin had met his in that public pool over twenty years ago.

Steve inched slowly toward the edge of the rock, careful to make no slightest sound. Leda was within a few feet of him now; he could hear her break stroke for a moment, probably to glance behind her and make sure her course was midway between the rock and the bank. And then the stroke started again, and Steve knew she was abreast of the rock. He filled his lungs silently, moved the last few inches to the edge of the rock, and started to submerge.

"Jimmy," Leda's voice said, almost in Steve's ear. "Jimmy, watch the rock."

Then another voice, a young boy's adolescent voice, seemingly only a few feet behind the girl. "Don't worry, kid. I've never hit it yet, have I?"

It took all the physical control Steve possessed to retain the air in his lungs and submerge. He sank slowly down into the soft warmth of the water, his muscles so tensed by surprise and anger that he could scarcely bend his knees.

He knew what had happened. Now, when it was too late, he knew it only too well. The boy Leda had spoken to in the water had been the one he had assumed had already started around the island before he got there. But he had been wrong; the boy must have slipped into the water at some time after Leda had swung out on the rope, and, swimming more rapidly that she, had almost caught up with her by the time she reached the rock.

Steve crouched on the bottom, staring up through the dark water, his anger threatening to expel the air from his lungs at any instant. A shapeless blob of whiteness drifted past above him, and his fingers ached with the frustrated urge to jerk the girl down to him anyhow—to kill her, just as he had planned to do. Then the whiteness passed and for long, lung-searing moments Steve waited for the next one. An eternity elapsed, and then the second body blurred dimly above him, and moved slowly away; and still Steve remained on the bottom.

He would never be able to stay under long enough, he realized; he had already held his breath longer than he had ever done before. Another ten, possibly fifteen seconds and he would have to come up. And that would be too soon; neither Leda nor the boy would be more than a few yards away by then. They would be almost sure to see him, whether he surfaced here or at the bank.

There was only one possible answer: He must, somehow, reach the far side of the rock before his breath gave out; and the far side of the rock was at least a dozen feet away.

Getting as much leverage against the bottom as possible, he straightened his legs suddenly and started around the rock. He couldn't see the rock at all, from time to time he was forced to break his stroke long enough to make sure he wasn't veering too far away from it. He was not an accomplished underwater swimmer at best, and judging distance beneath the surface had always been difficult for him, even when the water had been clear and the sun directly above. Now, he found, he had no idea whether he had gone five feet, or ten, or even more.

There was only one thing to do: hold his breath until the last possible tortured instant, make sure he was still hugging the rock, and then come up and hope that he had swum far enough for the rock to shield him from Leda and the boy.

When the pain in his chest reached the point beyond endurance, and a sudden giddiness told him he was beginning to black out, he placed a hand over his nose and mouth, so that he wouldn't gasp too loudly, and raised his face above the surface of the water.

He was behind the rock, but he had made it by so narrow a margin that at first he thought he was not. The corner of the rock was still a few inches to the left of his face, but it bulged slightly midway along its side, and it was only this bulge that stood between him and the swimmers.

He filled his lungs with air and moved a yard to his left and stood there, leaning against the rock for support, his whole body shaking violently.

Minutes later, when Leda and the boy had disappeared around the far end of the island, Steve crossed to the bank, dried himself with his undershirt, and got into his clothes. Then, realizing that the first of the swimmers must be nearing the other end of the island, from which point they would be able to see him, he ran up the steep incline of the rise and down the other side to the place where he had hidden his car.

Once behind the wheel, he drove furiously, and it was only when he was on the outskirts of Garrensville that his anger began to abate and his body ceased its trembling.

CHAPTER EIGHT

It was after midnight when Steve reached the square and parked the car, and the streets were almost deserted. He felt the need of a drink more strongly than he had ever felt it before, and he walked directly to the bar where he had stalled with a beer while he waited for it to get dark.

There were only a few scattered customers at the bar now, and the jukebox was dark and silent. A shabbily dressed woman at the far end of the bar glared at Steve belligerently, cursed drunkenly, then went back to mumbling over her glass of beer. Steve took a stool near the door and ordered a rye and water.

The bartender was a hairless, heavy-set man with purpled pouches beneath his eyes and brown splotches on the backs of his hands. "I don't mean to rush you, buddy," he said, "but if you think you'll want another, you'd better order up. We'll be closing in a few minutes."

Steve nodded. "Make the next one a double," he said. "Straight."

The bartender reached for a pony glass, filled it, and put it down beside Steve's highball.

Steve drank the double, chased it with part of the highball, and lit a cigarette. He had to unwind, he knew; he was still so knotted up inside that his nerves felt as if they were going to break through his skin.

"Hard day?" the bartender asked.

"Plenty," Steve said.

"Well, you've got the right answer," the bartender said. "A few drinks after a hard day never hurt anybody." He raised the bottle over the pony glass and looked at Steve questioningly. "You want another, while I've still got the bottle out?"

"I thought you were closing in a few minutes."

"We are. But a man like you, he gets a lot of

mileage out of a few minutes." He put the bottle away and made a swipe at the bar with his cloth. "Just passing through?"

"No. I'm opening a music store here. A record shop."

The bartender nodded. "Seems I heard something about that. You must be the fella that's taking Nancy Wilson's place."

"That's right."

"Name's George Turner. What's yours?"

"Garrity," Steve said. "Steve."

"Uh-huh. Well, you ought to do real good, Mr. Garrity. That's something the town's needed for a long time. A music store. What with all the money the kids spend on records these days, you ought to turn a pretty nice dollar." He smiled. "And just offhand, judging from the way you polished off that rye, I'd say that I was in for a business boom myself."

Steve grinned. "You've got a nice bar here, George."

"Thanks. I try to keep it that way. This is a place you can bring your wife. That's the only kind of place I'd run." He glanced down the bar. "Hurry it up, boys. I'll be closing up any minute now." Neither the other men at the bar nor the lone woman paid the slightest attention to him.

Steve could feel the warmth of the double shot spreading out from his stomach, but the knotted feeling was still there, and his hand on the glass was not quite steady.

"Shame Nancy had to lose her gift shop, though," George said. "A real nice girl, that Nancy. I've known her ever since she come into the world."

Steve had been listening to the bartender with half an ear, but now he gave him his full attention. "I just met her this afternoon," he said carefully. "But I'll have to agree with you, George; she's certainly a very nice person. There's something about her. I don't know, she just seems to put you at your ease as soon as you meet her."

"That's Nancy, all right," George said. "And pretty, too. You should have seen her when she was in her teens. Of course, she's prettier'n hell right now, but in her teens she was really something."

"I can imagine," Steve said.

"Yes, indeed," George said, shaking his head reminiscently. "Really something. And she was never uppity, like they get sometimes. She was always just as sweet as she is right now." He lowered his voice and leaned on both elbows on the bar directly in front of Steve. "I guess you might have heard about how she's taking care of that niece of hers?"

Steve took a sip of his highball. "She did say something about it, yes," he said.

"Uh-huh. Well, you won't find many girls that'd do that. Not this day and age, you won't."

"That's for sure," Steve said.

"No, sir. Me, I don't know that Leda too well, but I seen her around enough to get me a pretty good idea. You ask me, I'd say she'd be a pretty hard one to handle. You get the same impression?"

"Well," Steve said, "I just talked to her a minute or so."

George glanced along the bar again. "Those lights are going out any second now, boys," he said loudly. Not one of the drinkers even glanced at him. "Yeah," he said, nodding slowly, "you ask me, I'd say Leda Noland would be a handful for most anybody."

Steve took another sip of his drink. "I really didn't notice her too closely," he said casually.

"Well, you take a better look next time. You'll see what I mean. She's got the devil in those gray eyes, that one."

Steve smiled. Blue, he thought; she's got *blue* eyes, you blind bastard.

"I don't know what you could expect, though," George said. "A girl needs a mother, and that's something Leda never had. Died when she was born."

Steve shook his head slowly. "Tough," he said.

"Yeah. But I'll tell you one thing. You can say what you want about Ed Noland, but you can't ever say he didn't do all he could for her. Why, he was father and mother and everything else to her. The way he worshipped her, you'd think the sun rose and set in her navel."

"It's hard for a man to raise a girl," Steve said. "You have to give a man a lot of credit for even trying."

"You sure do," George said. "And Ed Noland, he tried harder than most. There wasn't nothing he wouldn't do for her—just like there wasn't nothing he wouldn't do for her mother before her." He sighed. "And now look at him. He winds up in jail and his daughter won't even go to see him."

"George!" the middle-aged woman at the far end of the bar called thickly. "What'n hell does a lady have to do to get a drink around this lousy dump?"

"She comes back tomorrow and acts like one!" George yelled at her. Then he winked at Steve and lowered his voice again. "I reckon that ought to hold her for a while, eh, Mr. Garrity?"

Steve smiled and took a final deep inhale of his cigarette before he stubbed it out in a tray. "You know, George," he said, "that strikes me as a little odd."

"What does?"

"That a girl wouldn't go to see her own father."

"Oh," George said. "Yeah, it is odd, isn't it? But she won't. She's been over to the county seat just once since he's been there, and that's all. It's—well, you might almost say it's *unnatural*." He shook his head and moved down the bar, collecting the drinkers' glasses whether they were empty or not. "Everybody out," he said. "I mean it, boys. I'm closing up."

The middle-aged woman rose, glared at George, and walked unsteadily to the door. "Keep your damn beer, for all I give a damn," she said, and lurched outside. The male drinkers rose, almost in unison, removed their change from the bartop, turned, and filed out, without a word or glance for either George or one another.

Steve started to rise, then hesitated. He had to drag this out somehow. He couldn't leave now, not when George had just begun to open up about Leda and her father. He sensed that he was very close to pay dirt, and he didn't mean to let it fall through his fingers. A talkative small-town bartender was no rarity, of course, but George was more than that. He was a compulsive male gossip.

"Better finish that, Mr. Garrity," George said. "I'm beat. Damn car broke down yesterday, and that means I've got a two-mile walk ahead of me."

Steve drank the rest of his highball and pushed the glass away. "Not tonight, you haven't," he said. "My car's just down the street."

"Well, say, that's mighty nice of you. You sure I wouldn't be putting you out?"

"Not a bit," Steve said. "And besides, I feel a little restless. The drive will do me good."

In the car, he said, "I just can't understand it, George. I mean, that a girl would treat her father that way." Then he bit at his lip. That's right, he thought; be subtle about it. Drive a two-penny nail with a sledge hammer.

But George, apparently, noticed nothing at all. "To tell you the truth," he said, slumping down in the seat, "I wouldn't much want to go over there again myself. I went once, you know. Right after they took him away. I never saw such a change in a man in my life." He paused. "Old Ed, he was all down to skin and bones. He wouldn't hardly talk to me at all. Kept looking around him all the time, like maybe he was scared somebody was going to slip up on him and hear what he was saying."

"How long's he been there?" Steve asked.

"Couple of weeks," George said. "But you'd think it was a couple of years. Looks like a corpse. All gaunted up and hollow-eyed, and shaky as an old woman. Take it from me, Mr. Garrity, there's something eating the hell out of him. Something's got him so scared he's almost nuts."

"Can't he get out on bail?"

"He *could*, sure—but how would he raise twenty thousand?"

Steve whistled softly. "Twenty thousand! What'd he do to make them set it so high?"

"You got me," George said. "All I know for sure is that he took some money that didn't belong to him. From the insurance company he worked for. But they never keep much cash around a place like that, so it couldn't have been any great big amount he got away with, now could it?"

"It wouldn't seem likely," Steve said. "But even so, couldn't he return it? Lots of times embezzlers get off pretty easy, if they make restitution."

"That's another thing I can't understand," George said. "If he's still got the money he took, why don't he give it back and get himself off the hook?" He drew a cigar from his pocket, bit off the end, and then rolled it around in his mouth without lighting it. "You ask me, there's something mighty damn fishy about the whole thing. Ed and me, we haven't been so close these last few years, but he's the last man in the world I'd bet would turn out to be a thief. He isn't the kind that ever amounts to much in this world. But he has a heart bigger'n a house, and, like I said, there isn't anything he wouldn't do for that girl of his." He lighted the cigar and blew the smoke out through his nose. "It just beats me, Mr. Garrity. That's all I can say. It beats me."

"What'd he do?" Steve asked. "I mean, what kind of job did he have?"

"Nothing you'd go bragging about, I guess. He used to be a pretty good bookkeeper, once upon a time, but he kept getting fired from first one place and then another. Don't ask me why. I think maybe he was just getting a little old before his time. Anyhow, when he went to work for this insurance company, he was just what you might call a general officer worker. He did a little bit of everything, the way I hear it. It was just a job; it didn't pay him hardly anything."

The next corner was the one at which George had told Steve to turn right, but Steve speeded up as he came to it and drove past it. He wanted to prolong this conversation as long as possible.

"You overshot," George said. "You should have turned right back there."

"Sorry," Steve said. "I'll circle around."

"It's all right. I should have said something."

Steve smiled. "You'd think a good lawyer would be able to get Mr. Noland's bail reduced, wouldn't you?"

George snorted. "What lawyer? Ed won't even talk to one. Old Sam Einetz went all the way over to the county seat, just to offer his services for free. But you know what Ed did? He wouldn't even talk to him."

"That doesn't make a lot of sense," Steve said.

"Damn right it doesn't. Like I said, the whole thing's fishier than all hell."

Steve nodded. "I'll have to go along with you on that, George," he said. "Of course, I'm new here, and I don't know any more about it than what you've told me, but it certainly does sound exactly that way."

"Yeah," George said, and lapsed into silence.

Talk, damn you, Steve thought. You were talking

your stupid head off a few moments ago. Why stop now?

He turned right, drove to the next intersection, and turned right again; but still George said nothing, apparently lost in his own thoughts.

"Next street, isn't it, George?" Steve asked.

"Yeah," George said. "That's Hardesty. You turn left on Hardesty, and I'm the fourth house from the corner. Big white stucco on the other side of the street." He roused himself abruptly and laughed. "This'll kill you, Mr. Garrity. I live right next door to the chief of police. Can you tie that? Me, a bartender, right next door to Chief Stroder!"

"That's very funny," Steve said, and hoped his voice sounded as if he meant it. "Right next door to the chief of police. Well, what do you know?"

"I thought you'd get a kick out of it."

Steve drew to a stop in front of the stucco house and turned off the lights, hoping George would ask him inside for coffee or a drink.

George opened the door, got out, and then leaned in through the window to shake Steve's hand. "Much obliged," he said. "Next time you come in, have one on the house."

"Thanks," Steve said. "It's been nice meeting you, George."

"Likewise," George said. "Well, I guess I better be getting on inside, Mr. Garrity. Got to get my beauty sleep, you know." He guffawed, released Steve's hand from his moist grasp, and walked toward his house.

Steve frowned after him, cursing him silently; then he dried his hand against his trouser leg, put the car in gear, and headed back in the direction of the square.

His was the only car on the streets, but he drove past the darkened houses slowly, trying to read some sense into the things George had told him. But it was almost impossible; none of the things made any sense in themselves, much less in combination with others.

By the time he had reached his hotel room and stripped and lain down on the bed, he had given up trying. The only thing that stood out clearly in his mind was the picture of Leda Noland's silvered naked body as it swung out and up and then hung suspended for a moment before it dropped suddenly down into the moonlit waters of the lake where he had tried to kill her.

That's all I need, he thought. Just let me get a real good letch for her. That's all it would take.

But he couldn't force the picture from his mind; and when, hours later, he finally fell asleep, it was still there.

CHAPTER NINE

At ten o'clock the next morning Steve finished his coffee at the soda fountain in the drugstore a few doors from his hotel and went back to the phone booth to call Nancy Wilson. The unfamiliar sensation of the morning sun against his eyelids had awakened him shortly after seven, and he had been unable to go back to sleep. He had shaved and showered, and then spent a full two hours lying on his bed with his fingers laced behind his head, trying to devise some new approach to Leda Noland's accident. But the more he turned the problem over and over in his mind, the more he became convinced that his only possible approach to Leda lay through Nancy Wilson. It was only through Nancy that he could even so much as talk to Leda without attracting the wrong kind of attention; and it was only by seeing Nancy as much as possible that he could hope to learn anything at all about Leda's habits, which, in turn, might suggest a way to kill her.

But just a business relationship with Nancy

wasn't going to be enough, not by any means. There was a definite limit to the contact he could wring out of a business relationship; he had, in fact, very nearly exhausted it already. What he needed was a completely plausible excuse for being around Nancy a great deal of the time, not only before Leda's accident, but after it. For as long a time after it as seemed necessary. It was important and as inescapable as his cover story about the music shop, his reason for being in Garrensville in the first place. At the time of Leda's death, and after it, everyone must associate him with Nancy so naturally and so strongly that there would be no chance of their associating him with Leda at all.

And that meant there was only one answer. He would have to romance Nancy Wilson, beginning now and continuing until he was beyond any danger whatever. He would have to lay siege to her with everything in the book. If she was receptive to his efforts, fine; he could manage her with only a part of his mind, while he reserved the greater part of it to cope with the problem of Leda's accident. If she repulsed him at first, fine; he would work all the harder; he would be the most persistent suitor she'd ever had. But the main thing was to give the town something to talk about, something to focus its interest on, something to divert its attention from his real objective. One way or another, the town was going to think of Steve-and-Nancy, not Steve-and-Leda; and if anyone—that Del character, for instance—got in the way, it was going to be just very much too bad. But not for Steve Garrity.

Now, as he dialed Nancy's number and listened to it ring, he tried to clear his mind of everything except the role he expected to play and the way he meant to play it.

"Hello?"

"Steve Garrity, Nancy," he said. "I hope I didn't wake you up again."

She laughed. "No, Steve, not this time. We've been up for hours."

"I was thinking of asking Mr. Runyons to give me an estimate on the work I'll need done at the shop. But I don't have a key to let him in, and I was wondering whether it would be all right to stop by and pick one up."

"Of course, Steve. How stupid of me! I should have given you the key when I gave you the receipt."

"Okay to come out, then?"

"Surely. Any time at all."

"Good. I'll be right out." He hung up, stopped at the tobacco counter to buy a pack of cigarettes, and walked down the street to the place where he had left the Ford. Things were looking up a little, he reflected. Nancy's voice had sounded light, almost gay; and she had said that she and Leda had been up for hours, which meant that Leda would be there, too.

Nancy met him at the door. "Come in, Steve," she said warmly. "Have you had breakfast?" There was a lilt in her voice, her gray eyes were bright and alive, and her heavy sheaf of auburn hair had been brushed until it shimmered. She was wearing a thin peasant blouse that exposed all of one shoulder and most of the other, a pleated white skirt, and black patent-leather pumps without stockings.

"Well, yes," Steve said. "But a second cup of coffee would go good."

She nodded. "I was just thinking of having another myself. Sit down, Steve. We'll have it out here."

"Fine," Steve said, and sat down on the davenport.

Nancy left the room, and came back almost immediately with two cups of coffee on a tray. "Cream and sugar?" she asked as she set the tray on the coffee table.

"No. Black."

She handed him his coffee and then moved to the chair nearest him and sat down, smiling at him over the rim of her cup as she sampled it. "Well," she said, as she put the cup in its saucer, "what do you think of our town by now, Steve?"

"I like it better all the time," he said. "Of course, I haven't seen very much of it yet, but what I've seen I like fine."

There was a movement of the drapes in the archway, and Leda came into the room. She was wearing blue jeans again, but the plaid shirt she'd worn yesterday had been replaced by a man's white shirt worn outside the jeans with the front of it reaching almost to her knees.

"Hello, Mr. Garrity," she said.

Steve nodded. "Good morning."

Nancy laughed. "If you're determined to dress that way, Leda," she said, "couldn't you at least find a smaller shirt?"

"No," Leda said, smiling faintly. "This was the smallest they had."

"You look lost in it," Nancy said.

Leda crossed to the piano bench and sat down. "That's the whole idea," she said. She swung her legs for a moment, looking at Steve. "Nancy says you play the piano," she said. "In some place in New York."

"Not any more," Steve said. "I'm an old man, Leda. I decided to give someone else a chance."

"You're not so old," she said solemnly. "I'd like to hear you play."

Steve smiled, glancing at Nancy, wondering about the subtle undertone in Leda's voice. It had been almost as if she'd said, "I dare you to *prove* you can play."

"Please do, Steve," Nancy said. "I'd like to hear you, too."

Steve shrugged, put down his cup, and walked to the piano. Leda moved down to one end of the wide bench, smiling a little, her eyes on the hands folded in her lap. Steve sat down beside her, rubbed the palms of his hands together to increase the circulation in his fingers, and grinned at her.

"What'll it be, Leda?" he asked.

"Anything," she said. "Just so long as it's fast."

Naturally, Steve thought. Of course. You want it fast. You equate the ability to play a lot of meaningless notes with the ability to play the piano, just the way most people do. It's a shame you've got so much to learn, kid, and so little time to learn it in.

"Well, who do you like?" he asked. "Wilson? Garner? Brubeck? Billy Taylor?"

"It doesn't matter," Leda said quietly. "Just play the way you always do."

He played one of his own favorite standards, "Sweet Georgia Brown," and he played it fast, keeping the tempo just this side of the limits of the piano and himself. He stayed with the melody only long enough to establish it, and then, still retaining the basic chord structure, piled improvisation on improvisation, increasing the volume of the bass figures gradually until the rhythm pounded through his arm and shoulder and set the old upright swaying on its feet. Then, abruptly, he dropped the bass to a whisper and let his right hand explode in a long series of figures that were as lyrical as they were difficult to execute.

From the corner of his eye he could see Leda's expression, and he smiled inwardly. She seemed to be holding her breath, her lips parted, her eyes rounded incredulously. She was, Steve knew, literally stunned.

He rose, trailing his left hand up the keyboard in a run, the way Tatum always used to do when he left the stand, and walked back to the davenport. Nancy was looking at him with an expression almost as incredulous as Leda's.

"Okay?" Steve said.

"I—I never heard anything like it," Nancy said. "I really had no idea that you were ..." She trailed off, flushing deeply.

Leda was still sitting on the piano bench, staring at the keyboard. "Thank you, Mr. Garrity," she said, and then got up and left the room without saying anything more and without glancing at either Steve or Nancy.

Steve watched her go and then looked questioningly at Nancy. "Looks like I drove her away," he said, making his voice sound amused.

Nancy laughed. "It certainly wasn't your piano playing. But I do think you've disappointed her a little."

"How so?"

"Well, she seems to think that all musicians should talk in a certain way. You know, use esoteric expressions and so on. 'Jive talk,' I think she called it."

Yes, Steve thought; that's just exactly what she would call it. "Most musicians do," he said. "Especially the younger ones. But it's usually only around other musicians."

"I see," Nancy said. "Leda was very curious about it. I think she hoped to pick up some new expressions from you to try out on the other kids." She glanced toward the drapes and smiled. "You know how they are at that age," she said in a lower voice. "Sometimes I have no idea at all what she's talking about. Honestly, the expressions some of them use nowadays! It's almost like some kind of foreign language."

"They're hard to keep up with, all right," Steve said, still trying to seem amused. Maybe, he thought. Maybe that was what was bugging her—and then again, maybe not. But there was no way to know for sure; and that meant there was no use in worrying about it—at least not yet.

Steve took a swallow of his coffee, but it had grown cold and he put the cup back again. "It's almost too nice a morning to waste on Mr. Runyons, Nancy," he said, smiling. "In fact, it's too nice a morning to waste, period."

"It is beautiful, isn't it? It's one of the loveliest days we've had all summer."

"Why don't we go for a drive or something? I can see Mr. Runyons this afternoon, or even tomorrow or the day after that. There's no real hurry at all."

He had expected her to refuse, or to give him the impression that she was thinking it over, or at least to be a little hesitant about it, but she surprised him.

"I'd love to, Steve," she said. "You're absolutely right; it's much too nice a morning to stay inside."

"Fine," Steve said. And then, throwing it away, "Maybe we should ask Leda. She might want to go with us."

"I'm sure she would," Nancy said, laughing, "but it seems she has a very important previous commitment."

"Too bad."

"The young man's name is Jimmy Miller. I understand he's one of our leading authorities on hot rods and so on."

"Oh. So it's like that." That damn Jimmy; he was probably the same boy Leda had spoken to in the water just a fraction of a second before Steve had got to her. But if that topless jalopy he'd been driving was a hot rod, then Steve's own car was a Jaguar.

"I have good news, Steve," Nancy said, her face radiant. "I feel I just have to tell everyone I meet."

"Oh? Well, tell me. I'm one of the best listeners you'll meet all day."

"I've got my teaching job back. They called me about it this morning, just before you phoned about the key."

"That's wonderful," Steve said warmly. "Congratulations."

"I'm so happy about it. I didn't realize I liked teaching so much until I tried something else. But I love children, and I've missed them terribly."

"I know what you mean," Steve said. "I feel the same way about kids myself. That really is good news, Nancy. I'm glad for you."

"Oh, and that reminds me. I've almost forgotten to give you your key again." She crossed to the library table and came back with a small brass key in the palm of her hand. "And once again, Steve—the best of luck."

Steve smiled, dropped the key into his pocket, and held the screen door for her. "All ready, Nancy?"

"How do I look?"

"Beautiful—and very, very happy."

She laughed. "I am happy, Steve. You've no idea what getting my teaching job back means to me."

In the car Steve started the motor and then said, "Any place in particular you'd like to go, Nancy?"

"Would you like to drive along the river?"

"River?" There was no river near Garrensville; he was sure of it.

"Well, it's hardly what most people would call a full-grown river. It's more of an oversized stream. But it's lovely down there. So cool and shady and all."

"Sounds perfect."

"Just keep on this street until you come to the highway, and then turn left."

Steve drove silently for a few moments, weighing one approach against another. Then he said, "I hope your friend doesn't object to this, Nancy."

She turned toward him. "Friend?"

"Del."

"Oh. Del. Have you—met him, Steve?"

"No." He smiled. "I just wouldn't want to cause you any more unpleasantness, Nancy, that's all."

Her face was sober now. "I'm very sorry about

that," she said. "Del is the one you noticed across from the shop."

"I guessed as much. That was some look he gave me."

"I'm really very sorry."

"Not that I blame him for being jealous."

The gray eyes clouded a little. "I must apologize for what happened. He called, and said he was coming right over, and—"

"I got the picture," Steve said. "And like I said, I don't blame him for being jealous. You're a very beautiful girl, Nancy."

"I'm twenty-seven, and I'm far from beautiful. But that isn't the point, Steve. I'm afraid you've got the wrong idea."

"Oh?"

"Yes. Del Strickland isn't my fiancé, or my boy friend, or anything else. He's just ... just a—"

"Just a guy?"

"No," she said angrily. "He's just an idiot! He— he's a *bully!*"

Steve nodded. "He did look a little rugged, now that you mention it."

"You still don't understand," Nancy said. "I've tried every way I know to make him leave me alone, but he just won't. I made the mistake of going out with him a few times last winter, and ever since then he's given me no peace. He keeps phoning and driving past the house in his car and picking fights with any man that even so much as smiles at me. He—" She broke off for a moment. "There's something wrong with him, Steve. He's sick somehow. He's vicious and brutal and—and I'm afraid of him."

"You been to the police?"

"No. What good would it do? Most of the things he does are things I couldn't prove. And besides, he's wealthy; he could buy his way out of almost anything."

"Sounds like he's got a pretty bad case on you."

"It's disgusting. He acts like—like a child."

"Maybe he needs someone to talk a little cold turkey to him."

"Everyone's afraid of him. I told you he was a bully. He's got everyone absolutely terrified of him, Steve. He can't seem to live without hurting people. Only a few weeks ago he got into a fight with two other men—very big men, too—and he put them both in the hospital."

"And the law didn't do anything to him?"

"Not a thing. The other men were afraid to press charges. Del paid their hospital bills and told them to hurry up and get well so he could put them back in again."

"Sounds like a real nice guy," Steve said evenly. "In fact, he sounds like someone I'd like to meet—uh—socially."

She glanced at him sharply. "What do you mean?"

To hell with subtlety, Steve reflected; it wasn't as if he had forever. "I guess you know my calling you about the key this morning was just an excuse, Nancy," he said. "It was a little crude, maybe, but it was all I could think of so early in the day."

She frowned. "I still don't follow you, Steve."

"Well, what I'm trying to say is that I wanted to see you. The key was only to give me a reason to call you in the first place." He paused, thinking his way ahead carefully. "And if I should get real lucky, and you should see me sometimes even without an excuse—well, I wouldn't want to think that somebody like this Del Strickland was going to be around to sour things up for us."

He didn't look at her, yet in the corner of his eye was an image of her, and her face told him nothing at all. This was a crucial moment, he realized; the ball could bounce either way, or not bounce at all. Damn it, he thought, why couldn't there be time to do this right? Slow and easy and subtly, with just the right touches, the right production.

Nancy's eyes were straight ahead now, he saw, and her face was still expressionless. "I'm glad you told me, Steve," she said softly.

Steve took the first deep breath he had taken in almost a full minute. "I never was very much with words," he said. "A piano man ... well, I guess he gets pretty used to saying things with his hands.... Does that sound crazy, Nancy?"

"No," she said. "It doesn't sound crazy at all."

"Well, maybe not crazy, exactly. But pretty brassy, I guess. Pretty brassy for a man who ..." He let his voice trail off helplessly.

There was a flash of ivory-white thigh as she drew one leg up beneath her and turned to face him, her face flushed and at the same time grave. "Steve. Steve, I ..."

"Yes, Nancy?"

"I want you to be careful, Steve. Del isn't like anyone else you ever met."

"Neither are you," Steve said. "And I've met Del Strickland before, Nancy. I've met him in almost every little town I ever played in. I've met him in dance halls and in bars and on street corners time after time after time. I know him, Nancy; I knew him all the way through."

She studied his face for a moment, and slowly a soft smile came back to her lips and she shook her head. "You're really not afraid of him at all, are you?"

"No," Steve said. "Not at all."

"But—but you'll be careful?"

Steve smiled, trying to keep it a little grim. "That's a promise, Nancy." He reached out and put his hand on hers for a moment and then took it away. "But let's not spoil the day talking about him. Let's just say he's no longer a problem, and let it go at that."

She nodded and her smile brightened as she turned her head to look out the windshield for an instant. "We're almost to the highway. You turn left."

He slowed the car and turned, and then, a quarter mile farther on, turned again and followed a narrow winding road that led along the stream Nancy had first referred to as a river. It was as cool and shady as she had said it would be, and when he reached an opening in the willows that bordered the stream he turned off and drove down to the water's edge. Except for the sound of the water and a few birds in the trees on the other side of the road, there was nothing but silence. He set the hand brake and leaned back in the seat and offered Nancy a cigarette.

"No, thanks, Steve," she said. "I don't smoke." She sat watching the water for a moment, her eyes thoughtful. "It's so peaceful here," she said. "So peaceful, and so very much away from everything. Sometimes I drive out here and just sit and watch the water and try to think things out."

"What things, Nancy?"

"Oh, you know. Why it is that people always seem one way when they're really another, and why people can't do the things they want to do without always worrying about what somebody else will think or say about it. Why people just can't be themselves without always having ... Oh, I don't know, Steve— just things."

"I know what you mean about wanting to do something, and yet worrying about what somebody else will think about it," he said.

She smiled. "Really? You strike me as a man who'd always do pretty much what he wanted to."

She sank back against the seat and put both hands up to her hair in a feminine combing movement that raised the firm breasts beneath the peasant blouse and caused them to nipple so sharply against the sheer material that Steve realized for the first time that she was wearing no brassiere.

He sensed that the movement had not been unconscious, and the knowledge somehow surprised him. And now he remembered the things she had said just a few moments ago, and her words took on a new meaning.

My God, he thought. How stupid can you get? She cued me in and I didn't even hear her.

Nancy tilted her head back and rested it against the top of the seat and closed her eyes. "You didn't finish, Steve," she said softly.

"Finish what?"

"About wanting to do something. You didn't say what it was."

So there it is, he thought; the next thing to an engraved invitation.

He drew her to him and kissed her. She put her hands against his chest and moved her head from side to side in an effort to free her mouth, but he held her tightly, knowing this was sham, just another step in the ritual. Then, abruptly, the pressure of her hands went away and her arms came up around his neck and the lips beneath his own parted hungrily.

He kept one arm around her and cupped one breast in the palm of his hand and felt the nipple stiffen against his palm; and then Nancy pulled away from him and tugged the blouse back up on her shoulder again and sat there with her face in her hands, breathing raggedly. "No," she murmured. "No, Steve."

"I'm sorry," he said contritely. "Believe me, Nancy, I—"

"No! That's not what I meant. I—I *wanted* you to."

He reached for her again, but she moved farther

away from him, still shielding her face with her hands. "It's this place," she said. "Someone might come by."

"No one's come by since we got here, Nancy."

"No, but they might. We've got to be so very careful, Steve. A woman in a town like this one has to—"

"We'll find another place."

She nodded eagerly, turning her body toward him but still not looking at him. "I know a place where we ..."

"Just tell me how to get there," Steve said, and started the motor.

They left the car at the foot of an impassable road, walked through a covered wooden bridge over what had once been a stream, and followed the same road along the side of a cliff to a grape arbor on what was obviously an abandoned farm.

The arbor was so thickly covered with vines that daylight penetrated only a few feet inside, and the ground was covered with a thick soft layer of fallen leaves.

Just inside the arbor Steve paused, thinking this was the place Nancy had had in mind, but she shook her head, grasped his arm firmly with both hands, and hurried him through the dimness of the arbor toward the patch of sunlight at the other end.

"This used to be my father's place," she said in her breathless voice. "This is where I grew up, Steve."

Steve said nothing. After his first instinctive reaction to a woman whose desire he had been able to arouse almost instantly, his own desire had subsided. It had always been that way with him. Whenever a woman had taken over the role he himself had expected to play, his need for her had almost invariably dissipated itself, and there had been times when he had even become completely impotent.

Now, as Nancy hurried him through the grape arbor, he felt the sense of wrongness, of vague apprehensiveness, that he always experienced when control of a situation had been wrested from his hands and there was no apparent way to recapture it.

They came out in a small grassy clearing completely surrounded by trees and very tall bushes. The sun was directly above them now, and the baked grass glowed warmly in its rays.

Nancy stood very close to him, smiling up at him with bright lips that trembled even as she spoke to him. "This is the place, Steve," she said. "No one can see us here."

He nodded dumbly, glancing about the clearing, wondering why it was that Nancy had surprised him so profoundly. This was no unique experience, this abrupt hunger. It had happened many times before; only the details had varied. And yet she had surprised him, very nearly stunned him.

"When I was a very young girl," Nancy said, "I used to come here. This was my very own place, Steve. I'd come here when the sun was bright and take off my clothes and pretend people were hiding in the bushes, watching me. I did it all the time."

She undressed slowly, her eyes averted, watching his face through her lashes. When she was completely naked except for her pumps, she stood for a long moment, smiling at him; and then she sank down slowly on the grass and lay back and raised her arms to him.

"Hurry, Steve," she whispered. "Please hurry."

Chapter Ten

By the time Steve had taken Nancy home and driven back to the square, it was twenty minutes past three.

His response to Nancy Wilson, once she had tak-

en off her clothes and lain down in the clearing behind the grape arbor, had been so completely and
intensely male that he had exhausted both Nancy and
himself. And yet, during the final moments with Nancy, he had found himself imagining that she was Leda, and that it was Leda's lips that had moaned so
demandingly in his ear and Leda's small white teeth
that had bitten so abandonedly at his chin and neck
and shoulder.

Now, as he parked the Ford, he wondered how
he could have blinded himself to Nancy Wilson in the
first place; and the fact that he *had* blinded himself
irritated him. It was true that Nancy had acted deco-
rously, until that moment by the stream when she had
put her hands to her hair to flaunt her breasts; and it
was true that he had made a natural mistake in assuming that a small-town girl like Nancy, a kindergarten teacher in her middle twenties, would be more
susceptible to a slower romantic approach than to an
out-an-out effort to make her; and it was also true
that George Turner, the bartender, had characterized
her misleadingly. But none of this was an excuse for
the assumptions he had made. None of it reflected
much credit on a man with his hard-won experience
with women and his cynical attitude toward them.

And yet he had been unwilling to accept Nancy
as just another nympho. He'd been with too many of
them, exhausted himself with too many of them. It
was hard not to chalk it up to a natural male ego, but
it had seemed to him that Nancy had been waiting for
someone just like him—not in the sense of saving herself for him, but in the way a volcano might erupt
when exactly the right combination of factors happened to occur at exactly the right time; the way a
door might remain locked for years, awaiting a certain key.

The difference was important. If Nancy wasn't a
nympho—if what had begun by the stream and ended

behind the grape arbor had been triggered by something peculiar to Steve—then his relationship with
Nancy was as assured and as solid as it could possibly
be. But if she *was* a nympho, even a periodic one, he
might be in trouble. The competition for Nancy's
time would be so intense that Steve's own efforts, his
attempts to identify himself with her in the eyes of the
town, might be stymied by the sheer numbers of the
men in the parade.

Before he left the car he tried to remove a little
more of the ground-in dust that the knees of his trousers had acquired in the clearing, and then rubbed his
mouth hard with his handkerchief to be sure he had
eliminated the last traces of Nancy's lipstick. The
trouser knees bagged a little, and his sport shirt was
wrinkled and perspiration-soaked, but there was
nothing he could do about them here in the car.

He got out, walked to the haberdashery again,
and bought two more sport shirts and a pair of light-
weight gabardine slacks. The slacks broke a little over
his instep, but he had noticed that the men here in
Garrensville didn't seem to concern themselves very
much about such things, and he wore the slacks and
one of the sport shirts out of the store and left the
soiled trousers and sport shirt at a shop to be cleaned
and pressed. Neither Ollie nor Mrs. Conklin had seen
him leave the hotel earlier in the day; they wouldn't
know how he'd been dressed. Then, still carrying the
other sport shirt, he went into the restaurant where he
had had lunch and dinner yesterday. He had no appetite; eating was just something that had to be done
and got out of the way so that he could concentrate
on other things.

It was only when he had sat down and the waitress with the protuberant eyes and the knotted jaw
came up to him that he remembered making an after-
work date with her for the previous evening. What,
exactly, had he said to her? He couldn't recall. He'd

had no idea at all of following through with her, and he'd been so occupied with thoughts of killing Leda in the bathtub that he might have said almost anything. Not that he gave a damn about the waitress' feelings, of course; it was simply that antagonizing anyone, even this sorry bone-and-skin hash-slinger, was very poor policy.

So, then, what had he said to her? That he would be by when she got off work? No. Then, suddenly, he remembered: He'd said that he hoped he could get away by then. He had, almost instinctively, given himself an out.

He smiled up at the waitress. It was little things like this that you had to watch. Big things were all composed of little things; if you watched *all* the little things, the big things would take care of themselves. Fluff one of the little things and you could wind up dead.

"I came in to tell you how sorry I am about last night," he said. "A crazy thing happened. Just as I started over here, I—"

"Arlene," the waitress said, staring at him balefully. "Go on with your lie."

He laughed. "It's no lie, Arlene. I—"

"I know," she said. "Just as you started over here, something jumped right out of nowhere and bit you on the neck."

"Well, I'll admit it wasn't quite that serious, but—"

"Not a mosquito, though," she said, leaning closer to him. "Unless mosquitoes have all at once started wearing skirts and growing teeth." She slapped the menu down before Steve and shook her head. "It looks like you picked yourself a live one, mister. She sure gnawed your neck proper, and that's for cryin' sure."

Steve watched her as she moved away haughtily, and then he got up and back to the men's room to see for himself.

It was bad, all right. One of Nancy Wilson's love bites had left a discolored, tooth-marked bruise almost as large as a poker chip. It looked exactly like what it was and nothing else, and it was so far up on his neck that not even a dress-shirt collar would cover it.

Steve cursed and stalked out of the restaurant. He'd had experiences with love bites before; sometimes the discoloration remained for days. And this was the worst, the most obvious one he'd ever acquired.

It was another of the little things, he reflected, another of the ridiculous little things that he shouldn't have permitted to happen—just as the second-nature kidding about a date with that hag waitress had been something he shouldn't have permitted to happen.

There were, so far as he knew, only three things he could do about Nancy's love bite. He could cover it with a bandage, or hide it with one of the cosmetic preparations women used to mask blemishes, or he could say to hell with it.

He said to hell with it. He had no intention of wearing a bandage on his neck during the rest of his stay in Garrensville, and the trouble with cosmetic preparations was that they required still other cosmetics to hide the mask. And besides, what real difference did it make? People would not be long in crediting the bite to Nancy, of course; but all in all, maybe that was the best thing that could happen. He'd wanted the town to think of Steve-and-Nancy, hadn't he? Well, what would start them thinking faster and harder than a love bite?

He went into the drugstore, had two steak sandwiches and a glass of milk, and then went out and located the funeral home where Mrs. Conklin had said he would be able to find Ed Runyons. His cover story about opening a music shop needed shoring up, and talking to Runyons about the necessary carpentry work was one of the best ways to do it. The trick was to have Runyons give him an estimate and pay him for his time, and then stall off buying the material and starting the actual work. That shouldn't be too hard to do, provided he paid Runyons enough to keep him happy, and then worked out a delaying action until after Leda was dead and he could come up with a good reason for abandoning the idea entirely. That, too, should be fairly easy to do. He could think of at least half a dozen reasons why he might leave town without having opened the shop, or in fact without investing any more money in the cover than he already had. If his romance with Nancy Wilson developed as he hoped, he might even use that. He could, after a proper time had expired, stage such a stormy scene with her that he would be forced to leave Garrensville and his music shop behind, brokenhearted, unable to live in the same town with her.

In any event, leaving Garrensville behind him, without at the same time leaving too much of his money there, would be no problem at all.

The mortuary shared a small building with a retail furniture store. The frail woman behind the desk brushed imaginary dust from her black dress and led Steve through a door that opened on a room with two morgue tables and an ancient four-body refrigerator, and through the room to another door that opened on a shipping dock, which apparently served both the mortuary and the furniture store.

An old man in striped overalls and a baseball cap sat on an unpainted wooden coffin, staring at nothing.

"This is Mr. Runyons," the woman in the black dress said. "Mr. Runyons works here—sometimes."

The old man looked at the woman, looked at Steve, shook his head, and sighed. "It's getting so you can't rightly tell the customers from the help," he said.

The woman's expression didn't change. She turned, nodded crisply to Steve, and went back through the door.

Steve sat down on the coffin beside Runyons and leaned his elbows on his knees. "I was talking to Mrs. Conklin, over at the hotel," he said. "She tells me you're a pretty good carpenter."

"That so?" Runyons said. "She must be after something, then. That's the first good word she's had for anybody in the last three-four years." He sighed again and tugged at the visor of his baseball cap. "What can I do for you, son? I make coffins for poor folks that can't afford better. You ain't in the market, are you?"

Steve laughed. "I'm opening a music store here, Mr. Runyons. I'll need some carpentry."

He took Runyons to the gift shop and spent the better part of two hours with him, making it look good, pretending to take as much interest in the old man's estimates and suggestions as he would have done if he'd really meant to have him do the work. When Runyons had finished, Steve gave him fifteen dollars for his time and told him that he would look him up again as soon as he had found out definitely when his stock of records and sheet music would be received.

Runyons' jaw dropped and he shook his head. "Lordy. Fifteen bucks! Why, for just estimatin', most people don't pay me nothing at all. You want to know the truth, fifteen bucks is just three bucks less'n what I get at that undertaker's for a whole week's work."

"That isn't right, Mr. Runyons," Steve said. "There's a law against that sort of thing."

"Sure, there's a law. And there's a lot of old-timers just itchin' for the job, too. What're you gonna do?"

"Damn shame," Steve said.

"Yeah," Runyons said. "You know it." He looked yearningly across the street at the grimy plate-glass window of a bar. "Well, if that's all you need me for today, Mr. Garrity ..."

"I'll get in touch with you again very soon," Steve said, and walked back toward his hotel.

As he passed his Ford he heard his name called softly. There was a dark Olds parked next to the Ford, and behind the wheel sat Vince Licardi. Licardi was studying a road map, his lips pursed thoughtfully as he scratched at the short gray hair above his left ear.

Steve started toward him, but as he approached the window on Licardi's side of the Olds, Licardi shook his head almost imperceptibly. "Don't be stupid! Get in your car and follow me." He hadn't taken his eyes from the road map, and now he shook his head as if puzzled by it and leaned forward to put it in the glove compartment.

Steve walked around the Olds and got into his car and pretended to be searching through his billfold for something, not even glancing in Licardi's direction. When the Olds pulled away from the curb he waited for a few moments and then followed it.

Licardi drove several miles past the city limits, then turned off on the shoulder of the road and got out to raise the hood. Steve braked the Ford and walked around to where Licardi stood frowning at the motor.

"Anybody else stops, we cut out before they get over here," Licardi said. "A little motor trouble, but we got it fixed. We don't give nobody a close-up."

Steve nodded. "All right. So what's the trouble, Vince?"

"Plenty," Licardi said. He took out his handkerchief and sponged at the back of his thick neck where

sweat had turned the collar of his blue silk shirt almost black. "I had a hell of a time finding your car.
That's all I had to go by, and if there's one Ford like
yours in this town, there must be a couple hundred."

"How'd you know I brought it?"

"I checked with the garage. What'd you think?"
He spat at the motor and watched the spittle dry and
disappear. "Too bad this is a boosted car. I wouldn't
mind owning it."

"What's up, Vince? I thought you said I'd be on
my own."

"You are. I just came up for the ride." He spat at
the motor again. "There's been developments, Stevie.
You ain't got a few days, like I said. You got to pull
this thing off right away."

"What do they want from me? This is only the
second day I've been here."

"Don't give me a big argument. All I know's that
Leda's old man has gone stir simple or something.
He's yapping where it can hurt. The boys want the hit
stepped up."

"Just like that, eh?"

"Yeah. Just like that."

"They think it's easy? I had one break, and I
came within an ace of doing it, but—"

"Who cares what you came within an ace of?
There's only one thing anybody cares about, and
you'd better get around to it."

"Damn it, Vince, it's going to take time. It takes a
lot of time just to work out the cover. Don't they realize that?"

"Maybe you think they sent me all the way up
here just to change your diaper," Licardi said.
"What'n hell have you been doing?"

Steve told him, stating it as briefly as he could.

Licardi listened, frowning, then shrugged. "Well,
maybe you're smarter than I thought. That part about
using your own name is pretty good, I got to admit.

Using a phony tag would just be asking for it."

"Thanks, Vince. Those pats on the back help a lot."

"You think you can keep your nose clean?"

"What do you mean?"

"I mean about her old man and all. Never mind about him. You're supposed to be concentrating on this Leda, and nothing else. Got it?"

"Sure. I wouldn't have time for anything else, anyhow."

"I just thought I'd remind you, in case your nose had started to grow. You think you can take that kid tonight?"

"Tonight! I'll be lucky if I get to her before—"

"Never mind the luck. It's just a matter of figuring it out, ain't it?"

"Yes, but—"

"All right. So *figure*. The pressure's really on, Steve. The boys want some action, and they don't mean to wait." He glanced both ways along the road and then reached into his pocket and handed Steve a clipping from a newspaper. "A little something for you to read," he said. "Maybe it'll help to pass the time."

The clipping was a wire-service news story with a one-column cut of a man's head and shoulders. Steve glanced at the face without recognition and then read the story. It was date-lined Cleveland and recounted the finding by police of a man's body in the cellar of a condemned house on the outskirts of the city. The body had been there several days, and at first identification had been impossible because the man's hands had been cut off and his teeth knocked out. The story lauded the Cleveland police, who, without fingerprints and dental work to establish identification, had nevertheless identified him by tracing a pair of custom-made shoes to a shop in Columbus.

Steve skimmed the story again and frowned.

"So?" he said.

"Take a look at that guy in the picture," Licardi said. "You should have made him right off." He glanced both ways along the road again. "And hurry it up. Some nosy bastard'll be along here any minute now."

Steve shrugged and studied the dark, heavy-featured face more closely—and suddenly he remembered. He could almost hear the soft whispery voice telling him what he must do to escape the Missouri gas chamber, that he must kill the white-haired man at the roadhouse to cancel out the murder of Johnny Callan.

Licardi was smiling. "Lousy picture, ain't it? I almost didn't make him myself."

Steve stared at him. "What the hell, Vince?"

"Those Cleveland bulls did a good job on the make, though; that's one thing you got to hand them."

"Talk sense, Vince."

"Usually, you take a guy and cut off his hands and knock his teeth out and dump him naked in a cellar somewhere, you're pretty sure the bulls will chalk it up as a gang hit and let it go at that."

"Listen, Vince."

"So sweat. That's what they figured you'd do. This guy was a pretty good torpedo, Steve. Better'n you, by a damn sight. But he took too long on his last one. He stalled around. He was supposed to hit this girl that danced in a joint, but he kept putting it off, trying to get in a couple of times before it was too late. So it was him got hit, instead."

Steve took a deep breath, held it for a moment, then let it out slowly. "I don't need an object lesson, Vince," he said. "What I need is time."

"Time you ain't got," Licardi said. "That girl's got to be hit, and sudden." He lowered the hood and held out his hand. "Gimme."

Steve handed him the clipping and fumbled in his pack for a cigarette.

Licardi opened the door and stood smiling at Steve for a long moment. "That story didn't tell it all, Stevie," he said. "What it didn't tell was that the guy's hands and teeth got took care of *before* he was hit. That and some other things. The papers don't ever print stuff like that, tough. They figure most people would get too sick to their stomach. You take the average person, now. He reads about a guy getting roasted, just like at a barbecue, he don't like it one bit—especially if he reads it while he's eating breakfast." He laughed, slammed the door shut, and drove away.

Steve stood on the shoulder, watching the Olds until it was out of sight. Then he broke the cigarette between his fingers, flipped it away, and walked slowly back to his Ford.

CHAPTER ELEVEN

Steve reached his hotel just as the evening sun began to sink beyond the hills to the west. The first gray of twilight brought with it the dreaded feeling of unease, of complete aloneness, enhanced almost beyond endurance by the roadside meeting with Licardi and the knowledge of what had happened to the whispery-voiced man he had talked to on that rainy night in Missouri.

Ollie was behind the desk, his bellhop's cap set squarely on his gray head and his chinless face stained with sweat and beard stubble.

"Hello, Ollie," Steve said. "You running the place now, are you?"

"Just till the old heifer takes on a load of alfalfa," Ollie said.

Steve forced a smile. "Is that what heifers eat, Ollie? Alfalfa?"

"It must be what that one eats," Ollie said. "You know anything else would fat her up like that?"

"Not offhand," Steve said.

"Me neither. I got a message for you, Mr. Garrity. Nancy Wilson wants you should buzz her right away."

"Thanks, Ollie. When did she call?"

"About half an hour ago. Just after the old bossy went out to graze." He lifted a phone from beneath the desk and pushed it toward Steve. "You can use this, if you want," he said as he turned to the switchboard. "Save you a trip upstairs."

Steve picked up the handset. "It's four-seven-eight-one, Ollie?"

"Right," Ollie said.

Nancy's voice had the same lilt it had held when he'd called her that morning. "Steve, Nancy," he said. "Ollie tells me you called."

She laughed. "A couple of maidens in distress, Steve. Leda and I have this simply enormous steak, and we were wondering what in the world we were going to do with it. There's enough for six women, or for two women and one very large-sized man."

"A picture is beginning to form," Steve said.

"We really do need help, Steve. And if you haven't had dinner yet ..."

"I haven't," Steve said. "Can you hold the fort another fifteen minutes?"

"Just barely. Are you coming to the rescue?"

"I'm already on my way," Steve said, and hung up.

Ollie took off his earphones and shook his head. "I'll be God-damned," he said.

Steve grinned. "What's the matter?"

"Nothing," Ollie said. "I'll just be God-damned, that's all."

Nancy led him through the house and out into

the back yard.

"It's such a nice evening, I thought we'd have dinner out here," she said. Her face had a flushed, sated look, but otherwise there was nothing about either her appearance or her manner to indicate that those naked hours behind the grape arbor had been spent anywhere but in Steve's imagination.

The yard was separated from the adjoining ones by waist-high ornamental shrubbery and sloped gently toward a huge flower garden crowded with bird baths and white trelliswork. There was a wooden picnic table midway between the back porch and the flower garden, and just beyond the table were several metal lawn chairs arranged in a loose semicircle around the far side of a small fish pond. There were voices from beyond the hedges at either side of the yard and a drone of insects from the garden, and once again the summer air was heavy with the acrid-sweet scent of brush fires in the hills.

Nancy steered him to one of the chairs beside the pool, glanced about them to make sure no one would see, and then went up on her toes to kiss him quickly but very thoroughly.

"Sit here," she said. "Leda will be out in a moment."

"Where will you be?"

"I'll be broiling the steak, silly. Would you like a drink? I made a pitcher of Martinis."

"Put me down for one."

"I'll send it along with Leda." She pushed him down into the chair, and then stood before him, smiling. "But on second thought, I don't know whether leaving you and Leda alone together is the wise thing to do. Especially with a pitcher of Martinis."

"Oh? Why not?"

"I think she's getting a crush on you."

Steve grinned. "Well, good. I was beginning to think I'd lost my touch."

"I'm not fooling, Steve. She's asked me a million questions about you. And when she heard you were coming over for dinner, the first thing she did was put on a dress and ask to borrow a pair of my nylons." She shook her head solemnly. "It looks serious, Steve. This is the first time she's worn long stockings all summer, and it's practically the first time she's had on a dress."

"I guess I just don't know my own strength," Steve said. "You sure she hasn't been at that Martini pitcher?"

"You'd think so, from the look in her eye." She bent down to kiss him again and let her breast brush softly against his shoulder. "Just remember I saw you first, that's all."

"I'll remember."

"Maybe after dinner we could go for a drive." She flushed. "That is, if—"

"You practically took the words out of my mouth," Steve said, and then caught himself an instant before he added, And maybe Leda would like to go with us. It had been close. Too close. If he'd been as alert as he should have been, the words would never have formed themselves in his mind, much less come within a breath of being said.

"I've fixed baked potatoes and a salad," Nancy said. "How would you like your steak?"

"Well done," Steve said. Actually, he liked his steaks medium rare, but a well-done steak would give him just that many more minutes with Leda.

"I'll put it on now," Nancy said, turning back toward the house. "Mind you watch yourself with Leda, boy."

Steve sat and looked at the goldfish in the pond and waited. His mind seemed to be everywhere and nowhere. Nothing would hold still. Nothing was what it seemed to be. At a time when either his or Leda's life depended on the clarity of his thinking, he couldn't think at all. He could only sit and wait and feel the day dying about him while either his or Leda's life ticked away as slowly and surely as the watch on his wrist.

He saw Leda's shadow before he saw the girl herself, and he looked up quickly.

She was walking carefully, trying not to spill the contents of a large champagne glass. Her lips were set determinedly, but her eyes were smiling. "Nancy says you're to think of this as a man-size Martini glass," she said as she set the drink on the arm of Steve's chair. "It holds almost three times as much as a regular Martini glass—I measured it."

Steve nodded. "Let's hope I'm man enough for it. Thank you, Leda."

She sat down in the chair next to Steve's and crossed her legs. "You will be," she said. "And Nancy says to tell you there's more where that came from."

Steve tasted the Martini and nodded appreciatively, watching Leda from the corner of his eye. She was wearing a pink seersucker dress with a high neck and a short skirt, and her nylon-clad legs tapered gracefully to slender ankles and high-heeled shoes that seemed almost impossibly small. Her full lips were moist and very red, and her pageboyed hair hung to her shoulders like a soft brown cape.

"I'm glad you could come, Mr. Garrity," she said.

"So am I," Steve said. "It was nice of you and Nancy to ask me."

She leaned an elbow on the arm of her chair and put her chin in the palm of her hand and smiled. "I've been thinking about you a lot," she said. "Ever since I heard you play the piano."

"That right?"

"Yes. You're the best I ever heard."

"That's very kind of you, Leda. Thank you."

"It must be wonderful to be talented that way. I

mean, to be able to do something better than anybody else."

Steve laughed. "Well, I don't think I'd go so far as all that, Leda."

"I mean it. All my life I've wished I could sing or dance or something. But I can't. I mean, not really. Not any better than most other girls can."

"It takes time. What are you? Seventeen? That's pretty young to give up, isn't it?"

"I was fifteen last month."

Steve shook his head. "I would have sworn you were at least a couple of years older."

"I'm old enough to know I'm not talented. You have to be born that way, and I wasn't."

He smiled. "Well, I wouldn't let it worry me. You were born beautiful, and that's much more important. Give yourself another two or three years, Leda; you'll see what I mean." Think, he told himself. For God's sake, think! There has to be a way. You've got to *make* a way.

Leda's chin was still in her palm and her body was still turned toward Steve, but now she had lowered her eyes and was looking at the water.

"I used to dream about going to New York or Hollywood and becoming a dancer or an actress," she said. "But I have a different kind of dream now. I dream the same thing almost every night."

"What kind of dream, Leda?"

She laughed, almost without sound. "You'll probably think I'm crazy."

"Cross my heart."

She glanced at him quickly, then turned her eyes back to the pond. "It's about money," she said, spacing her words slowly, "I keep dreaming I've suddenly got hold of a lot of money. And it's always the same amount—forty thousand dollars."

"A nice round sum. But as long as you're about it, why don't you dream of a million?"

"I don't know. It's always forty thousand. And just when I get the money in my hands, something happens."

"I know. You wake up."

She turned her face toward him and shook her head. "No," she said. "What happens is, I get killed." Her eyes were on his, not blinking, not showing any expression whatever.

"Killed?" Steve said.

"Yes. A man comes and kills me."

"That's quite a dream, Leda."

"You haven't heard it all. Just before I die, the man bends down over me and tells me he's sorry. And do you know what I tell him?"

"What?"

"I tell him that I would have given him half the money not to kill me." She was studying Steve's face as if trying to memorize every pore. "And then the man is sorrier than ever, and he begins to cry. But it's too late, because I'm already dead."

Raising his drink to his lips without spilling it was one of the most difficult things Steve had ever tried to do. "That's quite a dream," he said again, surprised by the tolerant, faintly amused tone of his voice. "Why should this man want to kill you, Leda? Or did he say?"

"No. He never says a word. Not till just before I die."

"I see. And where did you get hold of all this money in the first place?" He forced himself to take a long, unhurried swallow of the Martini and set it down carefully on the arm of the chair. "That's quite a bundle, forty thousand."

The heavy, glistening hair had swung forward and she brushed it back quickly with the back of her hand. "That's why the man is always so sorry," she said. "If only he'd let me live, he'd have had half of it for himself."

"Somebody leave you the money in a will, or what?"

She smiled faintly. "A man gave it to me to keep for him," she said, staring down at the pond again. "It's an awful thing to dream about, Mr. Garrity. I wish I could dream about something else."

Steve started to raise his drink again, then decided not to risk it. "I can't say I blame you," he said.

"And the most awful thing about it is that I like the man. I mean, I'd like him if I met him some other way. And I think he'd like me, too—if things were different." She paused. "If only he'd stop a minute to listen to me, we might ..." She broke off and reached down to adjust the tops of her stockings. She wore round garters, rolled high on her thighs, and in the few brief instants that her skirt was up, Steve saw that the narrow dark bands were so taut that they were almost flush with the white skin above them.

Leda glanced at him and laughed. "You're not supposed to look," she said.

"About this dream," Steve said. "I—"

"Please. Let's not talk about it any more. I don't know what got me started on it to begin with."

Nancy came out on the back porch. "You out there," she called. "You in the pink dress. Come help me carry some of this stuff outside."

Leda rose, smoothed the skirt down over her hips, and started toward the house. "Her mistress' voice," she said over her shoulder. "You may as well sit down at the table, Mr. Garrity. Everything will be ready in a minute."

Steve watched her until the screen door closed behind her. Then he picked up his glass, carried it to the picnic table, and sat down heavily.

What the hell did it mean? She couldn't know. It wasn't possible. And yet she had made up that dream; she'd done everything but come right out and bribe him. She had, in effect, offered him twenty thousand dollars not to kill her. But if she really knew—if she wasn't merely shooting in the dark—would she take the chances she was taking? Wouldn't she have gone to the police, or run away, or done something, anything, to protect herself?

No, he decided; she couldn't know. She might suspect, but she couldn't know. It wasn't conceivable that she could sit there so coolly with a man she knew was going to kill her. No matter how many ways you looked at it, it simply didn't make sense. She must have a good reason to think that somebody was going to try to kill her; that much was obvious. But she couldn't know it was he. She had suspected him, just as she would have suspected any other stranger who had come on the scene as suddenly as he had, and she had tried to sound him out under the pretext of telling him a dream.

It had to be that way; no other answer was within reason. The question was, How had he come off? Had he satisfied her that he was what he had represented himself to be? Or had he given himself away somehow, through some wrongness of expression or voice or manner?

He lifted his glass and drank steadily until it was empty. When Leda had raised her skirt to adjust her stockings and caught him watching her, she had rebuked him gently in an amused, femininely chiding voice that had been edged with something very much like relief. And when she had started back to the house and spoken to him over her shoulder, she had sounded like anything but a young girl in fear of her life.

I must have put it over, he thought. If I hadn't, she couldn't have been that cool. No girl alive could have been—not even Leda.

He wiped the sweat from his forehead and went into the house to refill the champagne glass. Another triple Martini would help a lot. He'd have to sustain

his act throughout dinner, and he would need all the
help he could get.

Chapter Twelve

During dinner, Nancy chattered almost constantly, Leda listened to her politely and said very little,
and Steve finished most of the steak by himself. He
hadn't been hungry when he had arrived, and he'd
had no appetite at all after he had talked to Leda by
the pond, but eating gave him an excuse to limit his
conversation to an occasional yes or no. As he ate, he
tried desperately to think of people and places back in
New York, of musicians he had known years ago, or
everything and anything but Leda Noland. He knew
that, in general, the more feminine women were, the
more highly developed was their sensitivity to the
moods and motivations of others. They weren't born
with it, but they acquired it early and perfected it every day of their lives. But Leda had lived only a little
more than fifteen years; if he could free his mind of
her entirely, there would be nothing to alert her.

But although he tried all through the meal to
keep his thoughts away from her, they kept coming
back at shorter and shorter intervals until he could
think of nothing else.

She had said that a man had given her forty thousand dollars to keep for him. Assuming for the moment that that was true, then the man must have been
her father and the forty grand must have been the
money he had embezzled from the insurance company. But how did you go about embezzling that much
money from a small-town insurance company? From
a bank, yes; it would be peanuts. But an insurance
company? It didn't seem possible.

But supposing he'd managed to do it—why
would he have turned it over to Leda? And if he had
turned it over to her, then why didn't she use half of

it to bail him out of jail? George Turner, at the bar, had said that the bail was twenty grand, and that Leda wouldn't even go to see him. It just didn't add up. With her father in jail and forty thousand dollars hidden somewhere, and assuming that she really intended to keep the money for herself, why was she still hanging around? And if she knew her life was in danger—was sufficiently certain of it to make up that wacky dream—then why didn't she act that way? Why wasn't she scared?

"More steak, Steve?" Nancy asked.

"No, thanks," he said, holding up his hand protestingly. "I couldn't eat another bite with a gun at my back."

"Was it all right?"

"Perfect. I don't know when I've enjoyed a dinner as much as I have this one. A good steak and a couple of pretty girls to help you eat it is a hard combination to beat."

"I love to watch a man eat," Nancy said. "It's the only thing that makes cooking worth all the trouble."

Leda laughed. "Mr. Garrity did all right with those Martinis, too. I sneaked a taste of the one I took him down by the fish pond." She made a wry face "I don't see how he drank it. It was nearly all gin."

"That'll teach you," Nancy said "What time is it, Steve?"

He looked at his watch. "Almost eight-thirty."

Leda pushed her plate back and got to her feet. "I've got to run," she said, touching the sides of her mouth with her napkin. "Jimmy's supposed to pick me up at a quarter after."

"Something tells me he isn't going to make it," Nancy said.

" 'Bye," Leda said, and ran into the house.

Nancy smiled and made a helpless gesture with her hands. "That girl! Honestly. You ever see anything like her?"

"No," Steve said truthfully. "I never have."

"She's just at that age, you know. So grown-up one minute and so childlike the next. It's all a little bewildering. But fascinating too, don't you think?"

"Yes. Girls her age are very interesting. No matter what they do or say, it's always a surprise." He lit a cigarette and let the smoke trickle through his nose. Now that Leda had left them and it was almost dark, he should have begun to feel a little better. But he didn't. The hours were melting away all too rapidly, and there was nothing he could do to stop the clock.

From the street an unmuffled motor coughed and roared and then subsided to an angry snarl that faded quickly.

"That would be Jimmy's hot rod," Nancy said, laughing. "He must have an airplane motor in there. I'm always afraid that car's going to explode and kill everybody in it." She rose. "You want to help me carry these dishes into the house, Steve?"

In the kitchen he offered to assist with the washing and drying, but Nancy shook her head. "I know how men hate to do dishes," she said, and led him out to the living room. She sat down on the davenport, drew Steve down beside her, and touched his neck lightly with the tip of a finger.

"I wonder what Leda thought of your— souvenir," she said. "I didn't notice it until we were all at the table."

Steve had forgotten the love bite entirely. Apparently neither Licardi nor Ed Runyons had noticed it at all. "There isn't much I can do about it," he said. "She'll probably think I got it somewhere else."

"But that isn't what I *want* her to think," Nancy said. She twisted around so that she lay on the davenport with her head in his lap, and then reached up to draw his face down to hers. "That isn't what I want *anybody* to think, Steve."

The screen door thudded softly, and Nancy jerked up to a sitting position so suddenly that at first Steve could not see who had come in.

"Del!" Nancy said, getting to her feet. "How dare you! What's the meaning of this?"

Strickland leaned back against the doorjamb and smiled at her. Up close this way, he seemed even bigger than he had when he had glared at Steve from across the street. Beneath the tangle of blond hair his small-featured face had the raw look of unhealed sunburn, and his pale hooded eyes were bloodshot and unnaturally bright. He would, Steve judged, weigh in at about two-twenty; and if any of it was fat, it most certainly didn't show.

"Get out of here," Nancy said. "You must be drunk."

Strickland looked at Steve and winked. "Isn't that just like a woman, now? She takes one fast look at me, and right away she thinks I'm drunk."

"You *are* drunk," Nancy said. "You must be. Nobody but a drunk would break in here the way you did."

Strickland sighed and took a step toward her. "What're you so riled up about? You got a guilty conscience, maybe?"

"Get out!"

"I kind of wish you'd stop saying that, Nancy. You make me feel like I'm not welcome around here. It's almost like I'd interrupted something."

"Will you please leave?"

Strickland shrugged his heavy shoulders. "But I just got here, Nancy. Where's your manners? And besides, I want to meet your friend."

Steve got to his feet, making it slow and friendly. The urge to knock that stupid grin off Strickland's face was almost overpowering, but it was a luxury he could not afford. Trouble with Strickland might mean trouble with the police, and trouble with the police was something he had to avoid. Once the law got its eye on you, it kept it there.

Nancy stood with her arms akimbo, her lips compressed angrily, glancing first at Strickland and then at Steve.

"Well?" Strickland said. "You going to introduce us, or aren't you? You ashamed of him or something?"

"You're disgusting, Del." Nancy said tightly. "Simply disgusting."

"My name's Garrity," Steve said, offering his hand. "Call me Steve."

Strickland ignored Steve's hand, hooked his thumbs in his belt, and measured Steve with his eyes. "My last name's Strickland," he said. "But I guess Nancy's already told you that much."

Steve nodded, smiling. "Glad to know you, Mr. Strickland."

Strickland's grin widened. "Why?"

"Del," Nancy said. "Will you please ... Oh, what makes you this way?"

"I've been hearing quite a bit about you, Garrity," Strickland said. "A small town like this, news gets around fast." He winked. "I hear you get around pretty fast, yourself. I hear you've even been pinch-hitting for me with my girl here."

"Oh, God," Nancy said, and sat down suddenly on the davenport. "I'm *not* your girl, Del. Can't you get that through your head? I went out with you exactly four times, and that was way last winter. Why won't you leave me alone?"

"I'd like to do that little thing for you," Strickland said, "but I just can't seem to put my mind to it."

"I'll call the police," Nancy said.

"Call them," Strickland said. "Go ahead. See what it gets you."

"I mean it," Nancy said, her eyes flaring. "If

you're not out of this house in one minute, I'll call Chief Stroder."

"You see anybody stopping you?" Strickland said. "Go ahead." He turned his eyes back to Steve. "I got something to say to you, mister."

"I'm listening," Steve said.

"Not in here. Outside. I don't want a lot of interruptions by crazy females that don't know their own minds from one second to the next."

Steve shrugged and started for the door. "Anything you say."

Nancy bounded to her feet. "Steve!" she said. "You stay right here!"

"Don't carry on so much," Strickland said. "Nobody's gonna get hurt—yet. Garrity and me are just going to have a quiet little talk about a couple things that need talking about. Being a newcomer here and all, naturally he needs a little friendly advice." He brushed by Steve, opened the screen, and stepped out on the porch. "Coming, fella?"

Steve followed Strickland to a point halfway between the porch and the street, then stopped as Strickland turned to face him.

"I figure this is far enough," Strickland said, grinning. "I mean that two ways, Garrity. Far enough so Nancy can't hear us, and far enough for you to see where your car's parked so you can climb in it and get the hell out of here."

"Still," Steve said, "there's always the possibility that I might not want to."

"I wouldn't like to think so," Strickland said. "I wouldn't like to think you're so dumb you can't take a friendly warning." His voice was soft and flat and cold. "One warning's just about the most I ever give. You're getting off lucky."

"That's a matter of opinion," Steve said.

"It sure is. You ask some of the guys I put in the hospital. They'll give you an opinion, and damn fast."

He stepped close. "Maybe you want me to spell it out for you."

"Maybe so," Steve said. You can't afford to have this happen, he thought. What the hell's the matter with you? Why can't you use your head, and walk off while there's still time?

"I wouldn't push it too hard, fella," Strickland said. "You're beginning to annoy me a little."

"That so?"

"You're going to get in that damn car and you aren't coming back. You know why?"

"No. Why?"

"Because no smart-assed New Yorker is going to come up here and try to take over my woman on me." His voice had risen slightly, but he lowered it again almost instantly. "That girl's too good to spit on the likes of you, Garrity. Nobody's ever touched her, and nobody's ever going to. Nobody but me." He paused and tapped the tips of his fingers against Steve's chest. "You want to stay healthy, remember that."

"Sounds like you want to marry her," Steve said.

"That's right. And now shut up. I don't even like to hear you talking about her."

"May I say just one thing more?" Steve asked.

"What?"

Steve smiled. "Fug you," he said.

Strickland's first swing was, Steve realized, almost pure reflex action. The fist grazed the hair at his left temple, but it would not have landed solidly even if he had not moved his head the fraction of an inch he found necessary to dodge it completely.

But there was nothing reflexive about the looping haymaker that followed it. Strickland brought it up from the grass, telegraphing it so clumsily that it was even easier to avoid than the first had been.

As always happened in a fight, except for that fatal attack on Johnny Callan, Steve's first concern was for his hands. Bare fists broke easily and healed slowly; and if a fractured finger or knuckle should fail to mend properly, Steve's days as a piano man would be over forever.

But elbows were different. Steve feinted with his right hand and brought his left elbow up sharply beneath Strickland's chin. Strickland's head jerked back, and Steve sank his right fist into the softness of the other man's stomach, being careful to place the blow well beneath the breastbone, because a hand could shatter there as easily as it could against a chin.

Strickland gasped and bored in, but the blow to his stomach had brought his guard down long enough for Steve to drive an elbow to his throat. It was the kind of blow that could kill a man, and Steve had intentionally pulled it just enough to make sure that he wouldn't have Strickland's corpse on his hands.

Strickland sighed softly and his arms sank to his sides. He stumbled toward Steve blindly, and Steve moved aside to watch him fall. It would have been pleasant to bring up his knee and smash Strickland's face on its way to the ground; but he had heard shouts and the pound of running feet, and he wanted to emerge from this as nearly blameless as he could. That was why he had let Strickland swing at him twice before he tried to defend himself. He'd wanted any possible witnesses to see that Strickland was the aggressor, and now he wanted them to see that he'd only done what was necessary to defend himself from Strickland's attack.

He glanced about him. Considering that this was a residential neighborhood, the crowd that was gathering was a sizable one.

"It's Del Strickland," someone said. "Damn if he didn't finally get what was coming to him."

Someone else chuckled. "No, he didn't, either. He's still alive, isn't he?"

"Who's that man?" a woman's voice asked.

"Beats me," a man said. "But it sure looks like old Del should have picked on somebody else."

No one asked Steve any questions; no one said anything to him at all.

"Here come the cops," a man said. "Now how'd they get here so fast?"

Steve looked toward the street. A black-and-white cruiser had angled in at the curb and two uniformed policemen were coming up the flagstones.

Behind him, Nancy's voice said, "Steve! Steve, are you all right?"

He turned toward her, smiling. "Sure. Didn't you expect me to be?"

"I—I called the police, Steve. I wanted to keep this from happening. Are you sure you're all right?"

"Not a scratch," he said. "I told you he wasn't going to be a problem, didn't I? He just needed someone to talk a little of his own language to him. If he doesn't get the message this time, I can always talk a little more."

Strickland was trying to sit up, but he wasn't having much luck and nobody moved to help him.

The two policemen walked over to him, stood looking down at him for a moment, then smiled at each other and came over to Steve and Nancy.

"Evening, Miss Nancy," one of them said. The other smiled and nodded but said nothing.

"Good evening," Nancy said. "Harry, Roy—this is Mr. Garrity."

"Evening," the policemen said together.

"Evening," Steve said.

"Looks like we got here just a little too late," Roy said.

"Or a little too soon," Harry said. "You must be a pretty handy gent with your fists, Mr. Garrity. I've known Del Strickland ever since he was a pup, and this is the first time I remember ever seeing him down on the ground."

Roy nodded. "And just to think that if I hadn't been working a double shift tonight I'd have missed it. Just shows you how working long hours can pay a man off." He looked at Nancy. "Just exactly what happened, Miss Nancy?"

"Mr. Strickland came into the house without being asked, or even knocking. He became abusive. When he made Mr. Garrity go outside with him, I called the police station."

"You see the fight?"

"Yes. I was watching through the screen. Mr. Strickland tried to hit Mr. Garrity. He punched at him twice, and then ... then Mr. Garrity hit him back."

"Ah, yes. That he did." He glanced at Steve. "You got your car here, Mr. Garrity?"

"Yes."

"All right, Harry," Roy said. "Let's ask a couple of the others, just to make it look good on the report."

"It was all his fault," Nancy said. "Mr. Strickland's, I mean."

"It always is," Roy said. "Harry, see if Strickland's in shape to ride downtown in the cruiser. If he is, drive him down and wait for me. I'll get a couple of fast statements from witnesses, and ride down with Mr. Garrity."

"Some passenger you're giving me," Harry said, and walked over to help Strickland to his feet.

On their way downtown, the policeman talked pleasantly of everything but Steve's fight with Strickland; and Steve stared glumly through the window, trying to explain to himself why he had permitted the fight to happen. It was almost as if he had been two persons, with one of them standing by helplessly while the other did his best to destroy both of them. He'd once read somewhere that some people carried so much guilt about with them that they were constantly doing things for which they knew they would be punished, because they felt they *should* be punished, unconsciously *wanted* to be punished.

Then there was that other theory, that some people wanted to die, but didn't realize it, and as a result were continually involving themselves in situations in which they could meet death, either at the hands of another person or by engaging in work or other activities so dangerous that death was a probability, or even by killing someone so that they themselves would be executed.

Bull, he thought. I know myself better than that. I don't feel any guilt at all, and I sure as hell don't want to die. It has to be something else that makes me do these things. If that was all there was behind it, I'd know about it, and I could control it. It wasn't guilt or a wish to die that made me drag Johnny Callan into that alley and beat him to death, was it?

Forget about it, he told himself. Why sweat? You don't know why, and you probably never will—and to hell with it.

He grinned mirthlessly. At least he'd succeeded in making the town think of Steve-and-Nancy. Although he hadn't realized it at the time, his fight with Strickland would be viewed by the town as a fight over Nancy; and that would identify him with Nancy more solidly than anything else he could have devised, no matter how long he worked at it.

"... Stroder," the policeman was saying.

"Excuse me," Steve said. "I guess my mind wandered off for a moment. What was that?"

"I was asking if you'd met Chief Stroder yet," Roy said.

"No."

"Thought maybe you might have heard of him, back in New York."

"In New York?"

"Yeah. The Chief's from there, you know. Used to be a pretty big muckymuck, before he retired and came up here. He was a detective with the Eighteenth Precinct for a long time, and then he was with the D.A.'s squad for four or five years. He's a damn good man. And I'm not saying that just because he's my boss, either."

"But why would he ... That is, why would a man—"

Roy laughed. "You mean what's he doing in a one-horse operation like we got here?"

"No. Nothing like that. I—"

"I know what you mean," Roy said. "Here's a man was a wheel in the biggest police force in the world, and he comes up here to an outfit that's only got a couple dozen men and one beat-up old cruiser. Sounds funny, huh?"

"Well ..."

"But not if you knew Chief Stroder. He's all cop, and nothing else. He's pushing sixty-five now, but he can work harder and longer than anybody else on the force. That's all he does do—work. Day and night. You might say he's—well, like a fanatic."

"That right?"

"Yeah, a real fanatic. I understand he was the same way in New York. His wife and little girl got killed, and it did something to him. Some guy he'd tracked down and put away. When the guy got out, he'd gone nuts. He went to Stroder's house to kill him for sending him up. But Stroder wasn't there, and so the nut just kills Stroder's wife and kid instead. You can imagine how that would hit a man."

Steve forced the word past his lips. "Yes."

"Damn right. And so Stroder couldn't stay retired. He tried it for a while, but it was no go. They couldn't take him on again in New York, because of the law they've got there about men his age, so he took this job here. He doesn't need the money, but he needs the work. Everything he makes he uses to buy equipment. For lab stuff and so on."

God, Steve thought. He couldn't be just another two-bit politician fronting up a hick police force. Oh, no. He had to be an ex-New York shrewdie with a God-damn mission. He had to be someone with a nine-foot monkey wrench, just waiting for a chance to throw it where it would do the most good.

"Well," Roy said, "here we are. Relax, Mr. Garrity. The Chief doesn't like Strickland any better than you do. Just watch your lip, and you'll make out fine." He led Steve into the police station and past the desk to a small alcove furnished with a table and half a dozen folding chairs.

"What happens now?" Steve asked.

"Wait here," Roy said. "You want to swear out a charge against Strickland?"

"No."

"Okay. It'd probably be a waste of time, anyhow. I'll be back in a minute."

Where were the other cop and Strickland? he wondered. Why hadn't he been taken immediately to the desk sergeant for booking, or for whatever else they meant to do with him, the way he would have been in New York? And if he had to waste any time in a cell, even so much as one night, what was that going to do to his chances of killing Leda Noland? Even provided he could carry it off, what would the syndicate bosses think of a man who would jeopardize the entire undertaking by getting into a senseless, needless fight simply because he hadn't enough self-control to walk away from it?

He lit a cigarette, took a few rapid puffs on it, then ground it out beneath his heel and began to pace back and forth across the narrow alcove. He'd screwed himself up again, but good.

A moment later Roy returned and took him down a short passageway to a door lettered: "CHIEF

OF POLICE—Emil Stroder." "Just remember what I told you about your lip," he said as he pushed the door open and stepped aside. "Everything'll be okay."

Steve nodded and walked into the small office, half expecting to find Strickland and the other policeman there, but they were not.

The man who sat on one corner of the ancient desk was as tall as Steve, and even wider through the shoulders. He had thick, carefully combed gray hair, a blunt-featured, wrinkleless face, and the wary, cynical eyes of the long-time cop.

"Garrity?"

"Yes, sir."

"Take the money out of your billfold, Garrity. Then hand me everything else."

Steve removed the money, handed the billfold to Stroder, and stood waiting. Stroder looked carefully at Steve's driver's license, his union card in Local 802, the miniature photostat of his honorable discharge from the Navy, his Blue Cross identification card; then he glanced hurriedly at the other cards and papers, replaced everything in the billfold, and handed it back to Steve.

"What's the address of the union hall, Garrity?"

"What?"

"The address of the musicians' local. What is it?"

"Two-sixty-one West Fifty-second Street."

"What's the serial number on your Navy discharge?"

"Six-o-three, six-two, five-five."

"All right, Garrity. Have a chair."

Steve slipped his billfold back in his pocket and sat down on a straight chair that was standing right beside the desk.

"I'm going to give you the picture," Stroder said. "Del Strickland isn't badly hurt, worse luck. He's down the hall, cooling off a little."

"I'm glad he's all right," Steve said. "Too bad I had to—"

"Just listen," Stroder said. "He started a fight, and got taken. If you want to, you can bring charges. Do you?"

"No. I'm just sorry it happened, that's all."

"If you did bring charges, it wouldn't accomplish anything. The most he'd get would be a fine. Fifty dollars or so. That's the way it is around here, Garrity. In New York, we'd book him on assault. But this is a country town. Fist fights around here are part of the way of life. You understand?"

"Yes, sir."

"Good. If we carried this through all the way, it'd mean a lot of headaches for everybody concerned. It'd be a hell of a lot of aggravation, and to no purpose. If we drop it—if we don't even put it on the blotter— you and Del can go home, and I can go back to work on something a hell of a lot more important than a brawl over a girl."

"That's fine with me," Steve said. "I haven't got anything against him at all. He was just jealous of Nancy and me, I guess."

"He's an authentic son of a bitch. He knows it, and he knows I know it. Maybe now he'll stop bothering Nancy. That's a fine girl, Garrity. What this world needs is more girls like her and fewer men like Del Strickland. Let's hope you taught him a lesson."

"Yes, sir."

"That's all. I hear you're opening a record shop here. Good luck with it."

"Thanks."

"On your way out, tell the officer who brought you here that I want to see him."

"Yes, sir," Steve said, and turned toward the door.

On the street, he started toward his car, then changed his mind and went into a candy store to call

Nancy and let her know what had happened. When he came out on the street again, he found Del Strickland leaning against the wall opposite the Ford.

Strickland smiled and put out his hand. "Shake, Garrity?"

"Sure," Steve said, but when he extended his own hand he kept his eyes on Strickland's, ready for anything Strickland might have in mind.

"This is just for the looks of it," Strickland said, still smiling. "Just in case somebody's watching."

"What's chewing you now, Strickland?"

Strickland pumped Steve's hand heartily. "You," he said. "I just wanted you to know that you and me have only started."

Steve withdrew his hand. "You want to pick it up again right now?"

"No. You took the first round. Okay. But don't think you're getting away with anything. I'm going to be laying for you, Garrity."

"You talk just like a kid," Steve said. "Get out of my way."

"One way or another, I'm going to get you, Garrity."

"Knock it off. I want to talk to kids, I'll look up a playground." He shouldered past Strickland and got into his car.

But Strickland's threat worried him. Not because he doubted his ability to handle Strickland physically, but because the big blond man was just wacky enough to start hounding him, watching his every move. And if that happened, it was going to be harder than ever to get to Leda Noland.

He started the motor so viciously that he almost killed it. He'd handled everything beautifully. He'd brought himself to the attention of the police, and he'd earned the blind hatred of a man who would probably stop at nothing to get even with him, and who would keep his eye on him from now on.

Steve was angrier with himself than he had ever been before. The syndicate had given him an almost impossible assignment to begin with, and he had made it even more so by his own lack of control in a situation that any sane man could have handled easily.

There was only one consolation. Using his real name and background ever since he arrived in Garrensville had paid off, just as he had thought it might. It had saved his life. If he had used an alias and a phony background, Chief Stroder would have found him out. He wouldn't have been able to go through with Leda Noland's murder—and that, of course, would have made him a walking dead man, just waiting for the syndicate to make it official.

Chapter Thirteen

Although Steve had left a call at the desk for eight o'clock, his phone did not ring the next morning until a quarter past ten.

"Sorry I flubbed your call, Mr. Garrity," Ollie said. "The old heifer was up on her high horse first thing this morning. She got me so flustered I just couldn't think right."

Steve kept the anger from his voice. "Forget it, Ollie. I needed the extra sleep anyhow."

"Sure hope I didn't mess up anything for you."

"No. It's perfectly all right, Ollie. Thanks for the call." He hung up, resisting the urge to slam the phone in Ollie's ear, and went into the bathroom.

When he had finished shaving he took one of the new sport shirts from the dresser drawer and walked to the window while he buttoned it down the front.

It was another beautiful day, just like the one before, and for a moment he stood watching the cars moving in and out of the big parking lot below, envying the people whose only immediate problem was a trip to the supermarket or the auto appliance store.

A new Cadillac pulled away from the brick wall to the left, and Steve's fingers paused on the final button of the sport shirt. In the parking space just beyond the one where the Cadillac had been was the topless jalopy that he had followed from the movie house to the lake. There was a girl in the back seat, and although he could see only her legs, there was no more possibility of mistaking them than there was of mistaking the jalopy itself.

It was Leda, he knew. She was lying in the back seat with her ankles crossed on the top of the door, all but her legs and plaid-trimmed shorts cut off from Steve's sight by the angle of his view.

As he watched, Jimmy Miller came around the corner from the appliance store and crossed to the front of the car. Leda got out of the back seat and walked around to join him. Jimmy showed her something he had been carrying in a small pasteboard carton, and then unscrewed the radiator cap and replaced it with another, much larger one from the carton.

Steve waited no longer. He scooped his keys from the top of the dresser, slammed the door shut behind him, and went down the steps two at a time. Less than three minutes later he had circled the block and pulled to a stop on the same side of the street as the parking lot.

If Leda and Jimmy went somewhere this time, and if they didn't pick up any friends along the way, Steve reasoned he would have a far better chance of getting Leda alone than he'd had the night he followed her to the lake. She and Jimmy might even go to the lake again; and if they did, and swam around the island the same way they had before, there would be another chance to drown her, even in broad daylight. It would be a tremendous risk, but he would have to take it. Time was running out.

For ten anxious minutes he sat waiting, wondering whether they might not already have left the parking lot before he got there. Then the jalopy roared through the entrance, turned right, and picked up speed.

Once again the jalopy moved out onto the highway, and once again Steve kept as far back as he could and let several other cars get between the jalopy and himself. But it was much more difficult to trail the car in the daytime than it had been at night, and when the jalopy started around curves—which meant that the occupants would be able to see all the cars following them at a glance—Steve reduced his speed until the jalopy was completely out of sight.

Then the jalopy turned off onto the same road that Steve and Nancy had traveled from the stream to the grape arbor, and a few moments later turned into a dirt road just a few yards beyond the impassable road where Steve and Nancy had left the Ford.

It would be impossible to follow them any farther without being seen, Steve realized, and he speeded past the road and up the curving hill beyond it.

At the top of the hill, he slowed and looked down in the direction of the grape arbor. He couldn't see the arbor at all, but he could see the top of the covered wooden bridge beyond it, and as his own motor idled he could hear the unmuffled motor of the jalopy echo hollowly through the bridge and then surge suddenly into a roar as it emerged on the near side of the dry stream bed.

Steve remembered now that the impassable road where he and Nancy had left the car had become passable several yards farther on, and he knew that Jimmy must have crossed over to it at that point and followed it to the wooden bridge.

The sound of the jalopy's motor stopped abruptly, which meant that Jimmy had parked just the other side of the grape arbor. There was no other place for him to have parked, and there was no reason for Jimmy and Leda to have gone to the arbor or the small clearing behind it if they hadn't wanted the same privacy that Steve and Nancy had wanted the day before.

Steve drove off the road and into the brush and parked behind a wall of small, heavily leaved trees. Then, using the top of the covered bridge to fix direction, he started down the hill toward the place where he knew the grape arbor and clearing to be.

He misjudged his distance a little, and he reached the clearing almost before he was aware of it. If it hadn't been for the sound of Leda's voice, he would have emerged within two feet of the spot where she and Jimmy were lying. He pulled up short and eased himself to a prone position, surprised that the sound of his breathing hadn't given him away. Then, moving very slowly, he inched forward to the edge of the clearing and parted the bushes the width of a finger and lay motionless, so close to the tops of Leda's and Jimmy's heads that he could almost have reached out and touched them.

Jimmy had sun-bleached red hair and thin bony arms splotched with freckles. He was lying on his back and smoking a cigarette. Leda lay on her side, her face away from Steve. She was wearing a sleeveless white blouse and very brief shorts, and now she had rolled the legs of the shorts up about her hips so that the plaid trim was no longer visible. Her position emphasized the flare of her hips and drew the rolled-up cuffs of the shorts well above the tops of her thighs.

Jimmy turned to look at her a moment, then flipped his cigarette away and made an angry sound deep in his throat.

"What's the matter?" Leda asked sweetly.

"You know damn good and well what's the matter," Jimmy said in his cracked, adolescent voice.

"You're just driving me nuts, that's all."

"Oh? Well, whose fault is that? Did anybody say you have to come around all the time?"

"I'll tell you something," Jimmy said. "You should pull those shorts down."

"You don't have to look, do you?"

"Like hell I don't. How'm I gonna help it?"

"I just can't understand you, Jimmy. These shorts don't bother me at all."

"Well, they bother me. They bother me awful. I'll tell you something, Leda. You're one hell of a damn tease. You know that?"

"Am I?"

"You go in swimming mother-naked, and lay around here with your shorts up to your belly button, and Christ knows what all. But just let a guy try to cop a feel, and boy! What's wrong with you, anyhow?"

"Nothing," Leda said. "At least, nothing I can see at the moment."

"I'll tell you something. You should either pull those shorts down or take 'em off altogether."

"Oh. So now I should take them off. First you want me to pull them down, and they you want me to take them off. First you say I'm a tease, and then you say I should take my shorts off. What's the matter with you?"

"You'd take them off if we was going swimming at the lake."

"That's different."

"It is like hell different. So why won't you take them off here?"

"I wish you'd think of something else. Just for once. All you ever want to do is—"

"Listen. I'm just as human as the next guy. What do you want to drive me so nuts for?"

Leda sighed and rolled over on her back and put her hands behind her head. "You're impossible, Jimmy. You really are."

Jimmy frowned at her for a moment, then twisted around suddenly and kissed her. Leda lay without moving, her hands still behind her head.

"Damn it, anyhow," Jimmy said, and pushed his hand inside her blouse.

Leda jerked up to a sitting position. "Stop that!" she said, trying to pull his hand away. "Jimmy! You'll tear my blouse."

"To hell with your God-damn blouse," Jimmy said. He got his other arm around her and tried to force her head back to kiss her again.

"Stop it!" Leda gasped, struggling against him. "Stop it, I said!"

Jimmy threw one leg across her body, trying to push her back down. "I had all I can stand," he said raggedly. "This time I'm going to— *Jesus!*" There was a sound of rending cloth, and Jimmy sank back on his heels, his hand going to his face. There were four almost parallel bright red furrows where Leda's fingernails had gouged the flesh from just beneath his left eye to the ridge of his jaw.

"Just look what you did!" Leda said, coming to her knees. The blouse was ripped all the way to the top of her shorts, and the frothy white brassiere beneath it had parted at the narrow band in the middle. She held the blouse together with both hands, glaring at him. "Damn you! How can I go home like this? You even tore my bra."

Jimmy stared at the blood on his hand, then wiped it on his handkerchief and held the handkerchief pressed against his face. He looked at Leda as if he were seeing her for the first time.

"Jesus," he said softly. "Why'd you have to go and do that? I didn't mean anything. Honest, Leda, I just ... just ..." He got to his feet, walked slowly to the grape arbor, and sat down on the bench just inside it, his back to the clearing.

Leda took off the blouse, turned it inside out, and sat with it in her lap while she reached up to take a bobby pin from her hair. Then, drawing the tear together, she clamped it with the bobby pin and reached up for another.

To Steve, lying on his stomach, only a few feet beyond the girl's back, the possibilities inherent in this situation had occurred full-blown, all of a piece, the instant Jimmy sat down in the grape arbor. With Jimmy sulking in the arbor, his back to the clearing, and with Leda engrossed in repairing her blouse, all Steve needed to enable him to kill Leda and put the blame on Jimmy was a little luck and a fair-sized rock.

He could smash Leda's skull without a sound; her thick brown hair made that certain. There would be no footprints because the ground was hard and the grass covered it like a matted carpet. Just a silent swing of the rock, a careful retreat through the trees, a fast trip back to town, and he could start counting the days until he could go home to New York and the life Vince Licardi had interrupted two mornings ago.

He began to feel about on both sides of him for a rock. This was going to be a little tough on Jimmy Miller, of course. He'd never be able to convince anyone, even a shrewd cop like Chief Stroder, that his clawed face and Leda's torn clothing didn't add up to attempted rape and murder. The kid had had it; all the lawyers in the state wouldn't be able to pull him out.

Steve's fingers had brushed against several rocks, but none of them had been large enough. Now he found one that seemed exactly right. He took out his handkerchief, grasped the rock with it, and came up to a kneeling position less than an arm's length behind Leda's back. He glanced at Jimmy to make sure he was still looking in the other direction, and then began to raise the rock, straightening his back to get the leverage he wanted.

The movement brushed his shoulder against the leaves of the bush beside him with a soft dry whisper that, even this close to his ear, was almost inaudible.

It didn't seem possible that Leda could have heard it, but she had. Her head whipped around so quickly that the blue eyes seemed to blur; then her body stiffened and her mouth flew open, and for an instant Steve thought she was going to scream.

But she did not. She darted back from the edge of the clearing and to her feet in one incredibly swift, continuous movement, holding the blouse up to her naked breasts, her lips starkly crimson against the sudden pallor of her face.

She couldn't see him now, Steve knew, and she wouldn't have been able to see the rock at all; he'd scarcely got it off the ground when she'd whirled toward him. But what difference did that make? He might just as well step out into the clearing and tell her the whole story. His mind raced, but for a moment his emotions seemed suspended entirely; he could think but he could not feel.

Leda was walking backward a little more slowly now, her eyes probing the brush to either side of Steve as if she expected to see someone else there.

Jimmy Miller still sat on the bench just inside the grape arbor, still holding the bloodstained handkerchief to his face, wholly unaware that anything had happened in the clearing only a few yards behind him. Leda glanced at him, seemed to be debating something for a moment, then turned her eyes back to the brush and finished slipping into her blouse. When she had buttoned it down the front, she stepped close to Jimmy and touched his shoulder. "I'm sorry, Jimmy," she said contritely, still glancing about the edges of the clearing. "I'm ready to go home now. Maybe Nancy won't be there and I can get out of this blouse before she sees."

Jimmy looked up at her and grinned. "Sure," he said. "I—I'm glad you aren't mad, Leda. I just sort of lost my head, I guess."

"I know," she said softly. "It was my fault, Jimmy."

"It's just that you're so pretty," Jimmy said. "Honest, Leda."

She took her eyes from the clearing long enough to smile at him. "It's all right, Jimmy. Really it is. But you'd better take me home now."

Steve watched them move off through the arbor; then he turned and hurried back up the hill to the road. His first impulse was to run—to run as fast and as far as he could. Run until his money gave out, and then sell the Ford and run some more. Run until the syndicate finally caught up with him and he turned into a handless, toothless piece of charred flesh in a cellar somewhere.

But he did not run. He raced the Ford back and forth along the highways for almost an hour, but he did not run. The speed of the car and the blurring roadside helped him think, and moment by moment his thoughts became more focused and coherent.

He'd panicked too quickly, he decided. He'd been so certain Leda had seen his face clearly, had known instantly why he was there, that he hadn't even stopped to consider the possibility that she had not. But he realized now that there was a very good chance that she had seen only part of a face, or part of a face and shoulder. After all, he had been well screened by the bushes, and the fact that he had been able to see her face clearly did not necessarily mean that she would have been able to see his own face equally well. His eyes had been only inches from the small break in the foliage, while hers had been almost three feet away; their positions had been somewhat like a man peering through a small crack in a door at a girl in the middle of a room. The girl would be able to see that there was someone there, and that it was probably a man, but that was all; she wouldn't be able to tell who he was.

Then there was the fact that Leda, after those first few seconds of alarm, had behaved very calmly. She had backed off warily, but she had not panicked. If she'd seen enough of his face to recognize him, she would have sensed the meaning of his presence and run screaming for her life. And then, too, there had been the way she had scanned the brush to either side of him, as if she had expected someone to be with him.

The only logical explanation for all of this, so far as Steve could see, was that Leda had assumed either that he was a Peeping Tom or that he had a girl with him, with the latter possibility being much the more likely of the two. Nancy had brought Steve to the clearing, just as Jimmy had brought Leda. The clearing was probably a well-known trysting place, employed at one time or another by most of the young people in Garrensville. If that were true, it might be that Leda had assumed that she and Jimmy had surprised another couple in the clearing, that the other couple had moved out into the bushes, and that either the man or the girl, or both, had slipped back to see what could be seen.

It almost had to be that way, Steve reasoned; nothing else made any sense at all.

Chapter Fourteen

By the time Steve got back to the square and parked his car, it was almost two o'clock. He had never felt less like eating, but he was beginning to experience the first stirrings of the nausea that always came when he went too long without food, and he walked to the drugstore and forced down two steak sandwiches and a malted milk with two raw eggs in it.

When he left the drugstore and turned in the direction of his hotel, Leda Noland stepped from between the opposing display windows of a hosiery shop and smiled at him.

"Hello, Mr. Garrity," she said, a little shyly. "I've been waiting for you." She was wearing a bright yellow dress with puffed sleeves and a full skirt, a pair of dark-gold nylons, and black, high-heeled pumps.

"It's always flattering to have a pretty girl waiting for you outside a drugstore," Steve said, trying to smile but not quite succeeding. "But why didn't you come inside?"

"There were too many people in there."

He shook his head. "Sounds very mysterious, if you ask me," he said, getting the smile on his face at last. "What's up?"

"Maybe we could talk in your car." There was a high color in her cheeks. "I mean, unless you're in a hurry to go somewhere or something."

"No," Steve said. "Let's go."

In the car, Leda sat very straight, her hands folded in her lap, smiling in Steve's general direction without quite looking at him. "You like Fords?" she asked.

"Always have," he said. "They're fine in traffic. And traffic's one thing New York has plenty of."

"Wouldn't you rather have a Cadillac?"

"No. If I wanted a Caddy, I'd buy one." He paused. "What's all this about cars, Leda? That isn't what you wanted to talk about, is it?"

She smoothed the yellow skirt out at each side of her and folded her hands in her lap again. "No," she said softly. "Not really. It's just that I can't think of how to begin."

"That's easy. Why don't you just begin at the beginning?"

"I don't know exactly where the beginning is."

"Well, start at the other end and work back."

"I'd be just as embarrassed, either way."

"Embarrassed?" He shook his head, smiling. "Girls confuse me sometimes, Leda."

She laughed. "Sometimes they even confuse themselves. At least, that's what Nancy says." She paused. "She wasn't home when I got there. I was just lucky."

"I'm still confused, Leda. Pretty girls confuse me even more than others."

"I mean she'd have been upset about my blouse. She'd have asked questions. It was lucky I got home before she did."

"Blouse?"

"The one Jimmy tore in the clearing," she said.

"Leda, do an old man a favor. Tell me what—"

"I saw you," she said, coloring more deeply. "Not Nancy, though. I knew she must have been out there with you, but I didn't see her at all." She glanced at him with mock reproach. "You should be ashamed of yourself, Mr. Garrity. You scared me half to death."

"Leda, so help me. I haven't the foggiest idea what you're talking about."

"I guess you got an eyeful, didn't you?"

"Leda, I—"

"I know," she said, laughing. "You think you have to be a gentleman and say it wasn't you. You want to protect Nancy."

Steve sighed, trying to look a little guilty, and said nothing.

"You like Nancy quite a bit, don't you?"

"I guess everyone does. She's a wonderful girl."

"That isn't what I meant. I wanted to know if you *liked* her."

"She's a very nice girl, Leda. Of course I like her."

"You think she's pretty?"

"Very pretty."

"Prettier than I am?"

"Well, that's hard to say. You and she are different types."

"But is she prettier?"

"No. I wouldn't say that."

"Do you think she has a cuter shape than I have?"

Steve laughed. "This is quite a third-degree. You mind telling me what you're getting at?"

Leda reached for the hem of her skirt and drew it up slowly until it rested a few inches above the taut dark bands of her garters. "Nancy says I shouldn't wear tight round garters like this," she said, looking at him along her eyes. "But I think they look lots nicer than the other kind. Don't you?"

"Well," Steve said, feeling the sweat beginning to lave his shoulders, "I really never thought very much about it, one way or the other."

"Do you think my legs are pretty? Prettier than Nancy's?"

"They're very pretty, Leda. But you'd better pull your skirt down. If someone should come by and look inside the car, they'd see."

She laughed and pushed her skirt down to her knees and sat there smiling at him. "Do you know what I wished when I knew you had Nancy out there—Steve?"

"No. What'd you wish?"

"I wished it wasn't Nancy out there at all. I wished it was me."

"You what?"

She lowered her eyes, but she was still smiling. "I wished it was me," she said. "And when I got over being scared, I was glad you'd seen me without—without my blouse on." She glanced at him, then looked away again. "I guess that's a pretty awful thing to say, isn't it?"

"I don't think Nancy would be very pleased to hear you saying such things, Leda."

"She hasn't got much room to talk, has she? I saw that mark she put on your neck. It's still there. A girl doesn't do something like that unless she ... Well, *you* know."

"Maybe I do," Steve said. "But you shouldn't. You shouldn't know about those things at all."

"I do, though," Leda said. "That's another thing I wish—that I'd put it there instead of Nancy."

"Seriously, Leda, you ought not to—"

"You saw me with Jimmy," she said. "That's what's wrong. He's nothing but a baby, and I treated him like one. And so you think that—"

"A baby? He's at least a year or so older than you are."

"Yes," she said, "but I'm a girl." She crossed her legs and leaned back against the cushion. "A woman, really. Hadn't you noticed?"

"No."

She sighed, reached for the hem of her skirt again, and drew it up almost to her hips. "Well, start noticing, then," she said, smiling serenely out the window. "When you make up your mind about me, let me know."

Steve lit a cigarette, drew the smoke deep into his lungs, and exhaled slowly, trying not to look at the swelling ivory thighs above the tops of the softly shimmering nylons.

This was danger in its purest form. The almost unbelievable violence of his physical reaction to Leda had alarmed him, and he knew how easy it would be for something like this to get out of hand. Whatever it was that girls had in their middle teens, and then lost forever, was the same thing that could short-circuit a man's reason just long enough to make him wish he were dead. Ever since a friend of his had been con-victed of statutory rape—even though the girl in-

volved had looked much older than seventeen and
was a proved prostitute—Steve had been reluctant to
be alone with underage girls any more than was absolutely necessary.

And if he weren't able to curb the consuming
young-girl hunger that he'd felt for Leda just now—
that he still felt for her—he wouldn't have to *wish* he
were dead; he would be it.

If this thing kept going the way it had started, the
whole town would know. Small towns always knew.
It would identify him with Leda, not Nancy. His
chances of killing Leda without drawing attention to
himself would disappear. And, back in New York,
someone would sign his death warrant.

"Well?" Leda said, still gazing serenely out the
window.

"All right," Steve said. "I'm convinced. Now put
your dress down."

"No. Not till you say my legs are prettier than
Nancy's."

"They're prettier. Pull it down, Leda."

She laughed, pushed the skirt down, and moved a
little closer to him. "Will you promise to treat me like
one from now on?" she asked. "Like a woman, I
mean."

"If that's what you want. But listen, Leda. We
can't—"

"Oh, but we can," she said happily. "We can if
we're very, very careful, Steve."

"You're only fifteen. I'm almost thirty-one."

"There you go again. That's just what I like
about us, don't you see? And besides, Carl was even
older than you. He was almost forty."

"Who's Carl?"

"A man I knew. I wouldn't say anything about
him, but I want to show you what I mean. This was
almost a year ago, so I was just a little over *four*teen.
We used to have dates all the time."

"My God."

"If you don't stop talking that way, I'll pull my dress up again."

"Forget I said anything. Go on."

"Well, he worked in this filling station, in Greenpoint. That's about twenty miles from here. He had a little room upstairs fixed up real nice with a studio couch and a record player and all, and I used to go there and stay with him all night."

"And Nancy never found out?"

"I wasn't living with Nancy then. I was still living with my father. But I have a girl friend in Greenpoint, and I'd tell him I was going to stay all night with her. This girl's mother works at night, and there isn't any telephone, and so I'd get off the bus in Greenpoint and fix things up with her and go down to the filling station."

Steve shook his head but said nothing.

"We could do the same thing," Leda said. "Only instead of the filling station, we could find somewhere else."

"No," Steve said. "Leda, you've got to realize—"

"But not all night," she said, ignoring him. "I could tell Nancy I was going to see a girl friend just for a few hours."

"No," Steve said.

"You're thinking about the way I was with Jimmy again. I wouldn't be that way with you, Steve. I'd be anything *but* that way."

"It isn't that," Steve said. "It's just that it isn't right, Leda. It isn't right for either one of us."

Her smiled wavered a little. "Steve ... don't you want to?"

"It isn't a matter of wanting to."

"Then what is it? I never got Carl into any trouble, Steve. I wouldn't you, either."

"But why not someone nearer your own age?"

"I told you. They're all babies. Unless it's somebody like you—somebody very big and a lot older and all—I just don't feel like doing ... like being with them at all."

"There must be at least five hundred men in Garrensville that would jump at the chance."

"But I wouldn't jump at them. Can't you see, Steve? It's not just somebody to be with; it's *you*." She shook her head. "I don't feel this way about just *every*body, Steve.... And besides, nobody else would be safe. They wouldn't know how to manage things. They'd get drunk and talk or something. That's why there hasn't been anybody else since Carl."

"And you think I'd be safe?"

"I know it. You're not like the men around here, Steve. It's like night and day."

There was a long silence.

"There's a bus stop near that place where you took Nancy today," Leda said. "Did you know that?"

"No."

"Well, there is. A Greyhound. It stops there so people can get off and take a little dinky old bus to Greenpoint. If Nancy wouldn't let me use her car, I could take the bus and get off and walk back to the same place you took her." She smiled. "Where you saw me without my blouse."

"And have half the kids in town walk in on us, I suppose?"

"No. Nobody else even knows about it except Nancy and Jimmy and me. And even Nancy wouldn't know if the farm it's on didn't use to belong to her father."

"There's still Jimmy."

"He wouldn't go there without me. He won't even look at another girl." She laughed. "He thinks he's in love with me."

Steve frowned, trying to hide his sudden surge of elation. This could be it, he knew; this could be the way Leda lost her life and he kept his own.

"We'd have to be careful," he said slowly. "If anyone caught us together like that, it would mean I'd go to prison. And you'd probably end up in a home somewhere. You know that, don't you?"

She nodded. "I know. It was the same with Carl. We can't even be seen talking together, Steve. I mean, not even on the street. This will have to be the last time that anyone even sees us say hello."

"It'll be hard to keep from Nancy."

"Not if I'm never gone too long at a time. She doesn't know a thing about me, Steve."

Steve smiled and dropped his hand to her thigh. "Neither did I," he said.

She put both hands on his and pressed his palm firmly against the hard narrow ridge of her garter. "I want you to know all there is to know about me, Steve," she said softly. "Everything."

The feel of the firm warm flesh beneath his hand made it impossible for him to think with any clarity, and he drew his hand away.

The more he turned the idea over in his mind, the more he became convinced that it was as solid as anything he could reasonably hope for. Everything depended on whether or not Leda came in Nancy's car. If she did, she would have her accident; if she came by bus, she would not.

"Why so quiet?" Leda said.

"I was just thinking. I'll have to keep on seeing Nancy, Leda. At least for a while. Just for the looks of things."

She nodded. "I guess maybe it would probably be safer that way."

"Yes."

"Poor Steve."

"Why?"

"Because after tomorrow night, you won't care whether you ever see her again or not. You won't even want to see her."

"What's wrong with tonight, Leda? Why wait till tomorrow?"

"I promised to help Nancy with her dresses. She's down at Copeland's now, buying gosh I don't know how many. She made me promise I'd model them for her tonight, so she can take them in or let them out or hem up the skirt a little, or whatever has to be done. You know how women do."

"But couldn't you help her some other night?"

She shook her head. "She's counting on me, Steve. She practically made me swear I'd be there. We're the same size, you see, and she—"

"But why the big rush? What difference would another night make?"

She smiled. "It's your own fault, in a way. She never paid much attention to herself before she met you. That's why she's over at Copeland's buying all those dresses, and that's why she's so anxious to get them all fixed up. She wants to look nice for you."

"She can't wear more than one dress at a time, can she? Why don't you help her with the one she wants to wear first, and then borrow her car and meet me at the grape arbor?"

"I couldn't, Steve. This is the first time she's ever asked me to do anything for her. She's been wonderful to me. If I tried to beg off tonight, she'd know it was because I was up to something. It—it wouldn't be *safe*, Steve."

"But, Leda ..."

"Please, Steve. I want to just as much as you do. But we just can't, that's all." She reached over and patted his hand, almost maternally. "And besides, tomorrow night'll be here almost before we know it. It'll be dark by nine o'clock. I'll be at the grape arbor between nine and nine-thirty; I promise."

"That's a long time," Steve said.

"It'll be just as long for me." She opened the door on her side of the car, glanced down at her knees to make sure they were covered by her skirt, and slid out of the seat.

"Between nine and nine-thirty," she said softly as she closed the door. "You won't be sorry, Steve—just wait and see."

She stepped up onto the sidewalk, smiled back at him, and started in the direction of the hosiery shop where he'd met her, walking slowly, glancing with feminine interest at the display windows she passed, seemingly oblivious of the suddenly stilled conversations about her and the heads that turned to follow her.

Steve dragged his eyes from the undulating hips beneath the yellow skirt and dug into his pocket for his car keys. Then, as he leaned forward to start the motor, he saw the burned paper match twisted into the slot of the ignition lock.

Licardi's signal that he had been there, and that Steve was to wait until he returned.

CHAPTER FIFTEEN

Steve did not have long to wait. He saw Licardi coming toward him along the sidewalk even as he flipped Licardi's burned match out the window. Licardi's round, jaundiced face was sheened with sweat and there were dark crescents of sweat beneath the arms of his light tan suit. It was the first time Steve had ever seen the short, fat-bodied man hurry, and it was the first time he had ever seen a worried look on his face.

Licardi stepped off the curb and walked between Steve's car and the one next to it. "The movie," he said without looking at Steve. "In the can. Five minutes."

Steve smoked a cigarette a quarter of the way down, then crossed the square, bought a ticket at the movie house, and went downstairs to the men's lounge.

Licardi was combing his hair in the mirror over the lavatories. "It's clear," he said. "I checked the stalls. And I could hear you come in the door on the other side of the lounge. Anybody else comes through, we can get shut up before they hear anything."

"Good."

Licardi slipped the comb into his pocket and turned around slowly. "You're a God-damned fool, Steve. You know that? You ain't got brain one."

"Never mind all the jazz. What's wrong?"

"You sitting there in your car with that chippy—*that's* what's wrong. I walked right past you twice, and you didn't even see me. You was too busy slobbering over her. You outa your mind?"

"It couldn't be helped."

"You're supposed to be trying to kill that girl, not trying to lay her. You stalling around trying to get in, or what?"

"Simmer down, Vince," Steve said. "What's up?"

"You futzed around too long, that's all. Now there's hell to pay." He jerked a paper towel from the holder and blotted the sweat from his face with it. "Her old man's gone nuts. He's like in a trance. The docs say that's the way he's going to be till he kicks off. Like a damn cabbage. We got a pipe into the county jail, just like we got one into the county attorney's office."

"So?"

"So the old guy didn't go nuts all at once. He did it gradual, and along the way somewhere he got to talking. He gave the law just enough to make it sure it was right about him in the first place. He ain't talking now, and he ain't ever going to be able to say another word, the docs say. But it's too late. What he didn't spill, that damn girl can."

"Back up a minute, Vince," Steve said. "I don't

even know what you're talking about. Remember? All you told me before was that her father was in jail."

"Yeah. Well, it's all different now. You're going to get the whole story. You know what they did?"

"Who?"

"The boys. They said that if you didn't hit that kid before tomorrow morning, you was dead. And that ain't all. They made me responsible for you. Whatever happens to you happens to me." He shook his head incredulously. "*Me*. You hear?"

"I hear you. But—"

"No buts. That's the way it is. You flub it, and we both get the treatment." He leaned a shoulder against the wall and stared at Steve with eyes that couldn't quite hide their fear. "Here's the pitch, just so you know what we're up against."

"Listen, Vince. Trying to get to that girl is like—"

"Stow it. *You* listen. I ain't going through this twice. You know why her old man's in jail? Because he knocked down damn near eight grand from an insurance company. You know who blew the whistle on him? Leda."

"*What?*"

"Yeah, Leda. That little armful you was slobbering over. She found out what her old man was up to, and so she blew the whistle and grabbed the dough. The trouble is, this insurance company is part of the operation. The boys are moving in around here, and they're using the company as a front. Strictly legit. But Leda's old man, he has to pull a little caper of his own. Lots of these farmers around here pay their premiums in cash, see? And they're big ones; the ones for dairy farms and vineyards and like that. So what does the old man do but take the cash and fix things up so it looks like it went back to the main office in New York. He must have been half nuts already, or he wouldn't even have tried it.

"All this I just found out myself, just before they

sent me up here with the word. When the crap really hit the fan was when they got the old guy in the county jail and the county attorney started squeezing him. First thing you know, they slap a twenty-thousand-dollar bail on him, just so they can keep him on ice while they work on him. This county attorney is smart as hell. He could smell the syndicate in there somewhere, and all at once he began to think of how it would be if he was governor. He wouldn't be the first that got there by busting up a little bit of the syndicate."

"Wait," Steve said. "You mean that Leda—"

"What's the matter? You don't hear good? She blew the whistle, I tell you. Her old man figured to steal a pile and then take her off somewhere and live good and send her to college and all." He turned to spit in the direction of the urinal. "That's funny, ain't it? The old guy worships the girl, see, and he sticks his neck out a mile just to make sure she has it good. And so what does she do but kick him in the teeth and yell for the law."

"But why?" Steve asked. "Why would she do it?"

"Who knows why? Who knows why a female does *any*thing? They spit on one guy and lay the next. They drown their own kid in a bathtub and run into a burning house to save a cat."

"You say this insurance company's legitimate?"

"Sure. But that don't mean the feds and the insurance investigators aren't going to shake it down. You think the feds are tough, you should tangle with insurance dicks. All the companies gang up and hire the best men they can find, and they'd spend a quarter-million bucks before they'd let anybody cheat a policy-holder out of a lousy dime. They have to. Just one case would be enough to give people such a scare that the companies would lose two or three times that much before the scare cooled off again."

"But if the company's legitimate—"

"Damn it, that ain't the point! Once this investigation gets rolling, it won't stop until some of the boys are in the soup. When they start going into the insurance company, they'll go into everything else at the same time. The company's only a wedge, like. They're just using it to pry the lid off the rest."

Steve nodded. "I'm beginning to get the picture."

"Those guys'll be here early tomorrow morning. The whole damn bunch of them. That's why you got to kill this Leda *tonight*."

"It can't be done, Vince. Not tonight!"

"Why can't it? It's got to be. Once those guys get their hands on her, she'll talk her head off."

"What makes you so sure she knows anything?"

"Our pipes in the jail and the county attorney's office. Who'd you think?"

"They could be wrong."

"They could, but they ain't. Leda's old man had big ears. He picked up a lot, and everything that went in his ears came right out his mouth. He wanted to be a big man in front of his kid, see? Maybe he had the hots for her himself or something."

"But the point is, she knows too much."

"Yeah—too *damn* much. Like I said, the boys are moving in around here. They're just using the insurance company as a cover—the same way you're using that record shop. But the same boys that are legit in the insurance company ain't legit anywhere else. They're digging in with the wineries and the dairies and the trucking outfits and so on. Once they get in solid enough, they can take over the crappy little unions and start raking it in from both directions. Either the guys in the unions will kick back part of their salary or they won't have any job. And either the guys that own the wineries and dairies and trucking outfits come through with the stuff under the table or they won't have anybody to work for them. Hell, there's all kinds of angles, once you get everything organized."

"But they haven't yet—is that it?"

"No. And you gotta remember that it ain't the in-surance company itself that these guys are itching about. It's the boys that run it. The boys can't stand any bright lights, if you know what I mean. They're not dug in enough. They haven't got the fix in solid enough. Once somebody turns on a light, it'll mean that the whole damn operation around here will be dead before it gets started. And some of the boys'll have their hides nailed to the door, sure as hell." He paused. "You think you got it all straight in your head now, or do you want I should do a recap for you?"

"I get it, so far. What I don't get is why Leda would talk. If she knows the kind of men she's up against, she must know what would happen to her if she—"

"Listen. She knows all this stuff, but she doesn't know what it means. She thinks the boys are two-bit punks, like her old man. The boys figured she must know plenty, or they wouldn't have sent you up here in the first place. But they didn't know just how much until the old man started yapping. Yesterday when I came up here, our pipe had just heard him say he'd told her some names."

"Names?"

"Yeah. Some of the biggest names in the outfit. Boys that are supposed to be completely legit."

"Around here?"

"No. In New York. That's why the boys sent me up here yesterday. They didn't know whether the old guy was telling the truth or not, but they wanted the hit moved up, just in case. And then, this morning, they found out he *was* telling the truth."

"How?"

"Because his Leda got on the long-distance and called one of the boys he'd told her about. That's how. She didn't come right out and try to blackmail him, but she sure didn't leave any doubt about what she was up to. I only got this conversation third or fourth hand, but—"

"Stop horsing me, Vince. Just because her father's crazy doesn't mean that she is. She's smart as they come. She wouldn't pull a stunt like that."

"No? You think I'm making this up just for kicks? If you do, you're as nuts as her old man." He shook his head. "It's like I told you. What she knows is names and facts and figures, but she don't know the whole story. If she did, she'd have better sense than to try a shakedown. It's like it is when you teach a little kid a dirty poem with a lot of big words in it. He don't know what it means, but he can recite it— and just because he doesn't know what it's all about don't mean that everybody else doesn't. Whatever this Leda knows, it's too much. And even if she doesn't know what all of it means, it won't make any difference. All she has to do is start yapping, and it's all over."

"But even without her, won't they—"

"No. They won't get *no*where. They ain't got enough to swing it. We got some lawyers coming up from New York tomorrow. Very expensive guys. If the kid's hit tonight, all they got to do is pay back the eight grand and make it look like the old guy was the only bad apple in the barrel."

"It's that simple, is it?"

"Nobody said it was simple. I'm just telling you how it'll wind up. If the county attorney and that bunch gets to Leda before we do, they win. If we get to her first, it'll give us a chance to fix things up so they can't hurt us. By the time they're ready to find out what Leda could have told them, it won't be there. Not a trace of it."

"And what happens to Leda if she doesn't get hit tonight?"

"You mean what happens to *us*. I don't have to tell you. You know damn well what'll happen. You forget that newspaper clipping already?"

"I was just curious."

"You got a feeling for the kid, maybe?"

"No."

"I think you're lying." He paused. "That's another funny thing. What would happen to her is nothing. She lives till tomorrow, she'll have her eight grand and all the fun of shooting her mouth off. Trouble is, you and I won't be around to congratulate her."

"You mean the syndicate wouldn't hit her at all?"

"For a stinking eight grand? You must be kidding. What'd be the percentage?"

"I thought maybe as an object lesson."

"For who? She ain't one of us. What'd hitting her buy the boys but more trouble than they already got?"

"You mean she'd get away with it completely?"

"Sure. Once she talked, they'd never touch her. It'd cause a stink all the way from here to New York. Hit her now, before she talks, and make it look like an accident, okay. They don't know we're on to her. It's just an accident—too bad. But hit her *afterward* and nobody would be fooled a damn bit. The boys would have hold of two tigers instead of just one."

Steve nodded. "I see."

"You better. I don't know about you, but I'm the type guy likes to die in bed, without no help from nobody."

From somewhere above them, Steve heard the music behind the picture build to the crescendo that signaled the end.

"All right," Licardi said. "I'm cutting out. There'll be a crowd leaving, now the movie's over. We space ourselves a few minutes apart. That way, maybe nobody notices we're the same two guys came in a while back."

"A hell of a lot that matters now," Steve said. "A hell of a lot anything matters now."

Licardi crossed to the door, then paused to look at Steve over his shoulder.

"You bring a gun?"

"No."

Licardi shook his head slowly, still unable to hide the fear that crawled in his eyes. "Too bad. If that girl ain't dead by tomorrow morning, you'll wish you had one."

"Why?"

"To use on yourself. Compared with what the boys'll do to you, shooting yourself in the head would be like scratching your finger."

Chapter Sixteen

Steve watched the door shut slowly on its pneumatic closer, and then stood very still in the tiled white silence of the men's room while he strove with every particle of will at his command to free his mind of everything but a single thought.

He must, somehow, get Leda Noland to meet him at the grape arbor, not tomorrow night, as she had promised, but tonight.

If he failed, there would be no tomorrow night.

He glanced at his watch. It was three-twenty. Leda had told him just a few minutes ago that Nancy had come downtown to shop for dresses at a place called Copeland's. That probably meant that Leda had come with Nancy, and that she had gone back to Copeland's to wait for Nancy to finish shopping, and then ride home with her. The girls might still be at store; and if they were, it was possible that he could talk to Leda alone long enough to persuade her to change the time of the meeting from tomorrow night to tonight.

He went upstairs, left the theater through a side exit, and walked around the square looking for a store called Copeland's.

This wasn't going to be easy, he knew. Even getting Leda away from Nancy would be difficult enough, and persuading her to meet him tonight would be much more so. He'd already pleaded with her, but she had been adamant about modeling Nancy's new dresses for her, and unless he could think of some compelling reason for her to change her mind, he would only appear ridiculous. He might even convince her he was too imprudent a man for her to risk meeting at all.

Maybe it would be better to work things from another angle. If he could devise some way to make Nancy postpone working on the dresses tonight, getting Leda to meet him at the grape arbor would be no problem. If he could, say, make a date with Nancy for dinner and a movie, she would naturally expect to be away from home most of the evening; she would put off having Leda help her with her dresses until another time. Or perhaps, if Steve could make the date with her right away, Nancy would hurry Leda home with her so that she could ready one of the dresses in time to go out. In either case, Leda would have her evening free. Steve could tell her what he had in mind, invent an excuse for taking Nancy home immediately after dinner, and then meet Leda at the grape arbor.

But first he would have to talk to both Leda and Nancy, and separately.

Copeland's turned out to be a small, shallow dress shop a few doors beyond the square. Steve glanced inside as he walked past, but he saw neither Leda nor Nancy, and when he looked at the cars parked along the curb he saw no sign of Nancy's Chevy coupe.

With the thought that they might be in one of the fitting rooms, he walked into the shop and asked the girl behind the cash register whether Nancy had been there. The girl told him that both girls had been in the shop for some time, and had left only a few minutes ago.

Then Steve recalled that when Leda had left the Ford, she had walked back in the direction of the hosiery shop near the drugstore where he had had lunch. He went to the hosiery shop, looked inside, and then walked completely around the square, hoping to see either the girls or the Chevy.

At ten minutes of four, he went into the drugstore and called Nancy's number. There was no answer. He came out and began a systematic canvass of the square, going into every women's shop he came to, but he saw neither girl.

At a quarter of five he tried Nancy's number again, then got into the Ford and cruised the streets until nearly five-thirty. Most of the stores and shops had closed now, and the streets and sidewalks were almost empty.

Finally he drove out to High Street and parked in front of Nancy's house. The shades were drawn and the front door was locked, but he knocked anyhow. When no one answered the door he sat on the top step of the porch and smoked a cigarette all the way down while he tried to dislodge the panic that was beginning to gnaw at the back of his mind.

"There's nobody home," a thin, whining voice said.

Steve looked at the heavy-set woman who had walked out into the yard at his left. She was about forty, with colorless hair and rimless glasses worn low on a sharp, high-bridged nose.

"I know," he said pleasantly. "I thought I'd wait a while."

The woman crossed her arms, stared at Steve challengingly, and raised her voice. "You know the people lives there, mister?"

"Yes," Steve said, smiling.

The woman narrowed her eyes suspiciously. "You sure about that?"

Steve nodded. "Of course."

"Well, they aren't home. Hard to tell when they'll be back." She looked meaningfully at the drawn blinds, and then glanced both ways along the sidewalk, as if she thought she might want to call for help and wanted to be sure it would be there. "Who'll I tell them was here?"

"That won't be necessary," Steve said. "I said I'd wait."

The woman opened her mouth, closed it again, spread her feet determinedly, and glared at him.

To hell with it, Steve thought. Another five seconds and the crazy bitch'll yelp for her husband to come scare the burglar away. And that's just what I need the least—a fracas with a couple of crackpot neighbors.

He smiled at her, got up, and walked down to his car.

As he started the motor he noticed the Pontiac parked across the street and saw that the man behind the wheel was Del Strickland. Strickland was looking straight ahead, his lips curled in a contemptuous smirk.

God, Steve thought as he drew away from the curb. Another one. Another crackpot.

Strickland was watching him, he knew, waiting for a chance to pay him back for the punishment Steve had given him in Nancy's front yard. If Strickland showed up at the wrong time tonight ...

He drove back to the square, parked near the hotel, and had two fast shots of rye at a bar before he went to the phone booth to try Nancy's number again. The booth was less than three feet from a pounding jukebox, and it was all Steve could do to hear the phone ring on the other end of the wire.

Leda's voice answered.

"This is Steve, Leda," he said.

"Hi."

"Where were you? I've been trying to phone your house all afternoon."

"Nancy didn't find everything she wanted at Copeland's, so we drove over to Greenpoint to see what they had there. We just got back."

"Can you talk a little louder, Leda?"

She laughed. "I'm already practically shouting. Is that your radio making all that awful racket?"

"No. I'm in a bar."

"Oh. Well, Nancy has the shower on full blast, and I can hardly hear *you*, either."

Steve pressed the receiver hard against his ear and put his hand over the other ear. "Maybe this is the best time to talk, then."

"With all the racket? You sound a little funny, Steve. Is anything wrong?"

"No. Not unless wanting to see you tonight is wrong."

"But Steve, we—"

"I know. But I think I've figured out a way to make it tonight. Can Nancy hear you?"

"Not in the shower. You can't hear anything at all in there."

"Good. I'll make it fast, before she turns it off." When he had finished telling her of his plan for meeting her after taking Nancy home from dinner, there was a long silence at the other end of the line. "Well?" Steve said at last. "What do you think?"

"I—I don't think it would work, Steve."

"Sure it would. Why wouldn't it?"

"I guess I'd better talk a little lower, just in case. Can you still hear me?"

"Yes. Why don't you think it would work, Leda?"

"Because she isn't that dumb. She isn't dumb at

all. You couldn't just invite her out for the evening, and then cut it off short like that. She—well, she'd *know*, that's all."

"How could she? And even if she did think something, she wouldn't connect it with you."

"You just don't know women, Steve. They don't think like men do. They—"

"Leda, I've just got to see you. Ever since you were in the car this afternoon, I've been thinking about you. I can't think about anything else."

"I guess I shouldn't have done what I did. I mean, with my skirt and all."

"It's just plain hell, Leda. You've no idea."

"Yes, I have, too. I—I feel the same way." She paused. "Poor Steve. You really do want to see me, don't you?"

"It's just got to be tonight, Leda. That's all there is to it."

There was another long silence.

"I'll try," Leda said. "But not the way you said, Steve. That way, we might just spoil everything."

"But you *will* meet me?"

"I said I'd try. I'll have to think of something."

"This other way would work. I know it would."

"No, Steve. *I* might be able to fool her, but you couldn't. Not that way. She thinks I'm still a child or something, so maybe I can get away with it. If I can only think of some way to—"

"But what if you can't?"

"Then I just can't, that's all. But I think I will. I feel like I've just got to see you, too, Steve. It—it's worse than it ever was with Carl. It's like I'm all on fire."

"Stop it, Leda. You don't know what that kind of talk does to me."

Another silence.

"I'll try," Leda said. "Honest, Steve. I'll try as hard as I can. If I can think of something, I'll meet you there as soon as it's dark. About nine. Maybe just a little after."

"Well, if that's the way you—"

"I'll have to hang up, Steve. She's turned off the shower."

"You'll do your best?"

"Yes, Steve. Oh, *yes!*" She was speaking softly now. "I'll tell her that it was Jimmy. 'Bye, Steve." The phone clicked off.

Steve went out to the bar and ordered another shot of rye. It was ten minutes past seven. Two hours to go. Two hours to wonder whether Leda would be able to come, and whether, if she was able to get away, she would come in the Chevy.

If she didn't bring the Chevy—if she had to come by bus—she might just as well not come at all.

Chapter Seventeen

Somehow Steve forced himself to remain in the bar until a quarter past eight. Then he walked out to his car and, taking the most circuitous route he could think of, drove to the road on the hill above the grape arbor and hid the car in the same place he had hidden it earlier in the day.

There was no moon, and it took him almost twenty minutes to find his way down the hill to the clearing and walk through the grape arbor to the near end of the covered bridge.

His eyes were becoming better conditioned to the darkness now, and he could discern the upper part of the cliff that fell away from the road between the bridge and the arbor. The distance between the edge of the road and the foot of the cliff was, he remembered, no less than twenty yards. Any car that left the road at this point would end up as a twisted mass of junk; there was no question about it. Not that the car's condition would make much difference. All that was necessary was that the car leave the road.

Satisfied that everything was as he remembered it, he walked back to the grape arbor, groped his way through the utter blackness to the middle of it, and sat down on one of the benches that ran along the sides to go over his plan once more.

If Leda brought the car, she would almost certainly approach the arbor by the same route Jimmy had used, which meant that Steve would be able to hear the car on the wooden bridge several minutes before Leda parked it and walked to the arbor.

The moment she stepped into the arbor, her death would be an accomplished fact. *If* she had brought the car. She would, the chances were, never even realize what had happened to her. All Steve had to do was break her neck, put her body in the car, and start the car rolling toward the edge of the cliff. When they found her, it would all be a tragic accident: A young girl had lost control of a car and ended up at the foot of a cliff with a battered body and a broken neck.

Steve flexed his long, muscular fingers. Breaking a small girl's neck was nothing, but breaking it quickly enough to prevent her clawing his face the way she had clawed Jimmy Miller's was something else again. It was the same kind of problem that had confronted him when he'd come so close to drowning her. And with a smart ex-New York detective like Emil Stroder to investigate her accident, it was equally important that she show no marks or bruises of a kind she would not be likely to receive in the accident itself.

The best way to kill her without marking either her or himself, Steve reasoned, was to wait until she was well within the darkness of the grape arbor. Then he could step behind her, pinion her arms against her sides, and with his free hand grasp her chin and snap her neck.

The rest would be child's play; a matter of

minutes. And neither the thick cushion of dead leaves inside the arbor nor the hard, rock-strewn road outside would reveal any trace of a struggle, even if there should be one. Just before he pushed the car over the side of the road, he would make certain that neither he nor Leda had dropped anything. Then he would start the car on its way down, run back up the hill to his own car, and be back in Garrensville within fifteen minutes. He would spend the rest of the evening in places where there were people to see him, and then, for once, go to bed with the feeling that this night was not his last.

And if Leda came by bus? If she didn't come at all?

But she *will*, he told himself again and again. She'll think of a way. She *has* to.

He struck a match, glanced at his watch, and blew the match out instantly. It was twelve minutes past nine. He put the match in his pocket and sat motionless, listening.

From beyond the covered bridge, the sound of a car motor grew louder, and then he could see the beams of the headlights tunneling through the bridge and he instinctively pressed back against the wall of vines and leaves.

The car came through the bridge slowly; then the headlights swerved sharply to the left, and a moment later they went off and the motor died.

Steve got to his feet and moved silently toward the end of the arbor. He could see nothing. The wall of night beyond the entrance was almost as black as the darkness within. He shifted his position until the backs of his calves were against the edge of the bench, and waited, his eyes straining toward the entrance.

There was the sound of a car door being closed gently and then the small sharp sounds of high heels on the rocky surface of the road. The heels grew louder, then faded abruptly, and Steve knew she was crossing the grass to the arbor.

There was a soft tinkle of bracelets, and he realized she was already inside. He could hear the sound of her breathing, hear the tiny rustle of her petticoat, smell the fragrance of her perfume. Then he saw, scarcely more than sensed, the almost invisible oval of her face, and he stepped forward.

She collapsed in his arms with no sound or movement other than the brief paroxysm of her body an instant after Steve broke her neck.

He lowered the small still body to the ground and placed the palm of his hand just beneath the swell of her left breast.

There was no heartbeat. She had died instantly.

Elation surged through Steve so suddenly and so strongly that he felt like shouting. He felt exactly as he had that night when he had been reprieved from execution in the Missouri gas chamber. In the utter darkness of the arbor he knew an exultation so intense that for several moments he was too weak to stand.

Then, slowly, strength flowed back into his limbs and he began to think again of what remained to be done. He had to work fast, and the first thing he must do was make sure that Leda had dropped nothing to indicate that she had left the car.

He lit a match—and suddenly his body froze and a cry tore its way through him and then died silently on his numbed lips.

The face that stared at him sightlessly in the flare of the match was not Leda's.

The girl he had murdered was Nancy Wilson.

Steve's acceptance of the fact that Leda had tricked him was much slower in coming to him than his realization of the fact itself. How long he knelt there beside Nancy Wilson's body while the knowledge curdled within him he did not know. But when at last he started to rise, and his hand brushed her arm, her skin was no longer warm.

Then, suddenly, he became aware that another car was approaching through the covered bridge, and he knew that he had been not only tricked, but trapped as well.

He cried out and turned to run, but his foot caught in the softness of Nancy's body and he stumbled and fell to his hands and knees. Before he could get to his feet again, a spotlight swept through the arbor, illuminating both Steve and his victim, and blinding Steve almost completely.

A shot rang out, a bullet tore through the leaves and vines above his head, and Chief Emil Stroder's voice thundered through the arbor. "Halt! One warning shot's all you'll get, Garrity!"

Steve stayed where he was, on his knees. Behind him a car door jerked open and feet thudded across the dead leaves.

"My God," Stroder said. "It's Nancy Wilson."

"She's dead?" another voice said.

There was a short silence.

"Yes," Stroder said. "Her neck's broken, Roy. Harry, put the cuffs on the son of a bitch."

Steve got slowly to his feet and turned around. Stroder was in civilian clothes; Roy and Harry were in uniform, as they had been the night Nancy had called them to stop the fight between Steve and Del Strickland.

Harry circled behind Steve, eyeing him warily. "In back," he said. "Put your hands in back of you."

Steve did as he was told and felt the metal bands close about his wrists.

Harry stepped around in front of him and took his revolver from its holster. He spun the cylinder with an oily, purring sound. "I hope you'll try to run, you bastard," he said. "I knew that girl since she was a kid, Garrity."

"Knock it off, Harry," Stroder said. "Get on the

radio and start an ambulance out here."

"I just this minute found her," Steve said. "I had a date with her here, and when I got here, I—"

"You're a lying son of a bitch," Stroder said. "You came back to finish what you started before you got scared off."

"No," Steve said. "Listen to me."

"We'll listen to you, don't worry," Roy said. "We'll listen real good." He turned to Stroder. "The guy's psycho, Chief. He'd have to be. If he wasn't, he wouldn't have come back."

Stroder nodded. "He's worse than psycho, Roy." He spoke quietly now, studying Steve's face as if trying to find something there he'd missed before. "Why *did* you come back, Garrity? You so anxious to rape a dead girl that you couldn't think straight? Didn't it even occur to you that they'd call the police and tell us there was a body here?"

"They?" Steve said. "What do you mean, 'they'? I don't know what you're talk—"

"Shut up," Stroder said in the same quiet voice. "We got a call, Garrity. A couple of kids came up here to neck a while, and they found the body. They wanted to do the right thing, but they didn't want anybody to know they'd been here, so one of them called us. The desk sergeant couldn't tell whether it was a girl or a very young guy. Or maybe it was somebody older, trying to sound like a kid. But no matter." He paused to glance down at Nancy's body and then back at Steve. "That was a good twenty minutes ago, Garrity."

"So what?" Steve said. "Is that supposed to prove something?"

"Not by itself, no. But you left your car in a bad place. The farmer that owns the property on the other side of the hill doesn't like people to use it as a parking lot. He found the car and called us. He'd got your name off the registration on the steering post."

"I told you I had a date with Nancy. Naturally, I—"

"But the farmer called us almost an hour ago." Stroder said. "It didn't take you all this time to walk down that little hill, did it, Garrity?"

"I was early," Steve said. "So I—"

"Stop it," Stroder said. "You came down here and tried to take it away from Nancy. When you couldn't get anywhere, you broke her neck. Then this other couple came along and scared you off before you could do anything to her. When they left, you came back to finish what you started."

"Jesus," Roy said softly. "What kind of God-damned fiend are you, Garrity? What kind of man kills a girl and then rapes her dead body?"

"I tell you I didn't do it!" Steve shouted. "I didn't even know she was here, until just a couple of minutes before you came. It was too dark in here. I came in and sat down and waited, and then I started to walk to the bridge to see if she was coming, and my foot touched something and—"

"And *crap*," Roy said. "Why'd you try to run?"

"Anybody would have run! I lost my head. I knew how it would look, and—"

"Shut up," Stroder said again. "I've been a cop all my life, Garrity. It's pretty hard to get me worked up about anything. But if you say one more word— just one—I'll personally kick your head off."

Harry came back from the cruiser. "Couldn't get the ambulance, Chief," he said. "But they'll send it out as soon as it gets back." He glared at Steve. "Run, you bastard. You started to once. Why don't you try it again?"

"Easy, Harry," Stroder said. "You stay here with the body. Roy and I'll take Garrity back in the cruiser."

"Bastard," Harry said tightly. "Why don't you run?"

"All right, Garrity," Stroder said. "Take a nice slow walk over to that car."

"Chief," Harry said, "give me just two minutes with him. Just thirty seconds, even."

"No," Stroder said. "You hear what I told you, Garrity? Start moving."

They walked to the cruiser. Roy got behind the wheel, while Stroder shoved Steve into the back seat and took out a short-barreled revolver.

"Don't tempt me," he said as he got in beside Steve. "Don't even open your mouth." He sat with the gun across his lap, its muzzle inches from Steve's stomach. "Roy, call the desk sergeant. Tell him I said to phone New York and ask them what they've got on Garrity. These sex boys have usually got a sheet longer than your arm."

"Check," Roy said, reaching for the handset mounted on the dashboard.

"And ask him to send somebody around for Nancy's niece— What's her name?"

"Leda," Roy said.

"Yes," Stroder said. "I remember now. Pretty tough on her. First her father gets himself in a jam, and now her aunt gets herself murdered."

"Yeah," Roy said, and began to talk into the handset.

Stroder leaned back and stared at Steve in the pale, sickly white of the dome light. "So you just had to come back," he said. "You couldn't help yourself, could you? You had to come back and do that to a dead girl."

CHAPTER EIGHTEEN

After Steve had been charged, searched, finger-printed, and photographed, he was handcuffed to a radiator in one corner of the muster room and ig-nored. With his free hand, he managed to light a cigarette, but the first lungful of smoke nauseated him and he threw the cigarette away. His teeth ached, and there was a white, cold pain behind his eyes. His chest felt constricted, as if there were something bound tightly about him from throat to stomach.

A few moments later Leda and a policeman Steve had not seen before came through the street door and walked toward the corridor that led to Stroder's private office. Leda was dressed just as she'd been that afternoon, but the yellow dress with the puffed sleeves looked as fresh as it had when she had met Steve outside the drugstore. She walked with her head down, a small yellow handkerchief to her face; and when she passed the place where Steve sat handcuffed to the radiator, he could see that there were tears in her eyes.

The minutes dragged by slowly. There was activity all about him, but no one said anything to him or even looked in his direction. Then he heard Leda's high heels coming back toward him, and he looked up.

She was with Chief Stroder, both hands holding tightly to his arm. She looked at Steve with tear-bright eyes and shook her head incredulously. "How—how could you?" she said, sobbing. "How could you *do* that to her, Mr. Garrity?"

Steve straightened in his chair, and Leda gasped and cringed back from him.

"It's all right, honey," Stroder said soothingly. "Just don't get too close to him, that's all."

"She—" Steve began.

"Shut up," Stroder said "That girl must have been in love with you, Garrity. Any girl that would agree to meet a man the way she did ..."

"She—she thought there was something funny about it," Leda said hoarsely. "But she went anyhow. She was crazy about him, Chief Stroder. She—she *trusted* him."

"Obviously," Stroder said. "Well, let's find you a place to wait, Leda. All this is likely to take some time."

She sank down on a chair a safe distance from Steve's. "I feel a little bit sick," she said. "I think maybe I'd better just sit here a while."

"Poor kid," Stroder said. "But watch you don't get any closer to him." He turned and walked back to the desk.

"You shouldn't have tried to kill me, Steve," Leda said softly, her face partly hidden by the handkerchief. "Now you'll go to the electric chair, won't you?"

Steve stared at her. The one eye he could see was smiling at him.

"Aren't you curious about how I knew?" she asked. "It was because you thought I was a drum majorette. But you were wrong. That outfit belonged to another girl. I just borrowed it to have my picture taken."

"I hope you're enjoying this."

"Oh, I am, Steve. Are you?"

"Go to hell."

"There was only one copy of that picture, Steve. Somebody stole it from my father's desk, after he went to jail. And then, when a complete stranger comes to the house and ..." She shrugged. "Well, what other answer could there be?"

"That wasn't enough. Not just the picture."

"No. But then I made up a dream for you. I wanted to see how you took it. Then I knew for sure. And there really is forty thousand dollars, Steve. Or there will be. I've already got eight thousand that my father hid in the cellar. I found it one night and kept after him till he told me where he got it. He stole it from his boss. So I turned him in and kept it for myself. And there's nothing anybody can do about it, either. They can't even prove I ever saw it."

"Congratulations."

"And with Nancy dead, I'll get her house and that store building. Altogether, it'll come to forty thousand—maybe more. Of course, I'll have to wait quite a while for the rest of it, but that's the way it was left in her father's will. It all comes to me."

"You aren't human, Leda," Steve said. "You can't be."

"You'd be surprised how funny that sounds, coming from you." She paused, glancing about her to make sure no one else was close enough to hear. "I was trying to think of some way to kill both of you. Then, when you tried to kill me at the grape arbor, I saw how I could get you to kill Nancy for me, and get rid of you at the same time. You gave me the idea yourself, Steve. I just don't know what I'he have done without you."

"God," Steve said. "Oh, God."

"Why did you think I teased you that way in the car? I was going to stall you off one more night, just to keep you from getting suspicious of me, and then send Nancy out there to meet you."

"God …"

"Then you said it had to be tonight. I knew I didn't have much time. So I told Nancy you had called and said you'd meet her in the 'secret place,' and that you couldn't be reached by phone but that you'd explain everything when she got there. I pretended I didn't know what you meant, and I kept after her to tell me, just to make it look good."

"You called the police," Steve said. "You told them where to find her."

"I told them where I *hoped* they'd find her. I just put myself in your place, Steve. I pretended I was you, and Leda was coming to meet me. It wasn't very hard to guess what you'd do." She lifted one shoulder in a tiny shrug. "And if things hadn't worked out the first time, they would have the next. I'd just have thought of some other way, that's all."

"Fifteen," Steve said dully. "A fifteen-year-old girl."

She smiled around her handkerchief. "This has been even more fun than I'd thought it would be. I've been looking forward to it ever since they came to tell me what you'd done to Nancy."

"I'm never going to the chair, Leda."

"No? What, then? An asylum?"

"Not that, either."

Neither of them said anything for almost a full minute. Then Leda stood up, turned her back to the room, and smiled.

"Did you like it in the car?" she asked. "I mean, what I did with my skirt and all?"

"Go to hell," Steve said.

She grasped the front of her dress as if she meant to raise her skirt for him, then pursed her lips and shook her head.

"No, I'd better not," she said. "I thought it would cheer you up a little, but Chief Stroder mightn't understand." She turned away, walked to the far side of the room, and sat down in a chair near the wall. A small, tearful girl with a handkerchief to her eyes.

She would get away with it, Steve knew. Nothing he could ever say would make any difference. In the eyes of Chief Stroder and everyone else, he was a madman, a sex fiend who'd murdered a girl and then came back to rape her dead body—a monster. No one would even listen to him, much less believe him.

Leda had won. She had outwitted him completely. She had turned his attempt on her life into a way to kill Nancy Wilson, get Nancy's property, and send Steve to the chair.

And, so far as the syndicate was concerned, Leda was as safe as she could possibly be. She'd be under Stroder's protection for the rest of the night; and tomorrow, after she'd told what she knew to the county attorney, the syndicate would never be able to touch her again.

The activity was being stepped up now. Other policemen were coming in. There were the sounds of an angry crowd forming in the street outside the police station.

Chief Stroder crossed to Steve and unlocked the handcuff from the radiator. He grasped the cuff in his hand and motioned Steve toward a stairway. "On your feet, Garrity," he said. "Make one false move and you're dead. You understand?"

Steve rose slowly—and then, with all the strength of his arm, he jerked the cuff from Stroder's hand and lunged across the room toward Leda Noland.

"Stop!" Stroder yelled. "Stop, God-damn you!"

Steve plunged on. "I'll take you with me!" he screamed at Leda. "I'll break your neck just like I—" Then Stroder's gun roared and a slug ripped through Steve's rib cage and he stumbled and almost fell down before he recovered his balance and charged toward the girl again.

Leda screamed and jumped to her feet—and then stood there, her body rigid, her eyes round with terror, and her red mouth working horribly, as if she were trying to scream again and could not.

Stroder's second bullet caught Steve at the base of the skull and tore away the left side of his forehead. Steve's body crashed headlong into Leda's, bowling her back and down in a swirl of nylons and white thighs and a yellow dress that was now streaked with red and gray.

For a long frozen moment there was no movement in the room, no sound of any kind. Then Stroder and the other policemen rushed to Leda, shoved Steve's body roughly away from hers, and helped her to her feet.

"Are you all right?" Stroder asked.

Leda swayed on her high heels, brushing futilely at the spreading stains on her dress. "Look at me!" she said angrily. "Look at what he did to my dress!"

"It's shock, Chief," Roy said. "She doesn't even know what she's saying."

Leda started. Then, slowly, she raised her tear-damp face to Stroder. There was no slightest trace of anger in the blue eyes now; they were wide and stunned and immense. She took two short, faltering steps toward Stroder; then Stroder held out his arms and she came into them and pressed her cheek hard against his chest.

"He—he tried to hurt me," she said in a small, frightened voice. "He tried to ... to hurt me."

Stroder stroked her hair, staring past her at the wet-red face of the big man on the floor.

"You poor kid," he said gently. "You poor little kid."

THE END

"Jonathan Craig" was born Frank Eugene Smith on May 14, 1919 in Lexington, Missouri. He first worked as a clerk for *The Kansas City Star* newspaper and then relocated to Washington, D.C., to take jobs with the U.S. government. During World War II he joined the navy where he was appointed as head research analyst for the Pentagon. After the war, Smith became an advisor to President Truman at the Potsdam Conference. He started writing in 1947, penning western and crime stories in a spare, sardonic style. His first novel was *Junkie!* in 1952. Smith went on to write a series of ten police procedurals featuring detectives Pete Selby and Stan Rayder during the 50s and 60s for Gold Medal Books. He died after a long illness in New Port Richey, Florida, on September 14, 1984.

JONATHAN CRAIG BIBLIOGRAPHY
(1919–1984)

Novels

Pete Selby/Stan Rayder Series

The Dead Darling (1955)
Morgue for Venus (1956)
Case of the Cold Coquette (1957)
The Case of the Beautiful Body (1957)
Case of the Petticoat Murder (1958)
Case of the Nervous Nude (1959)
Case of the Village Tramp (1959)
Case of the Laughing Virgin (1960)
Case of the Silent Stranger (1964)
Case of the Brazen Beauty (1966)

Stand-alone novels

Junkie (1952; reprinted as Frenzy, 1962)
Read-Headed Sinner (1953)
Alley Girl (1954; reprinted as The Renegade Cop,
1959)
Come Night, Come Evil (1957)
So Young, So Wicked (1957)
Quadroon (1970)

Gothic novels as by Jennifer Hale

Stormhaven (1970)
Ravensridge (1971)
House of Strangers (1972)
The Secret of Devil's Cave (1973)
The House on Key Diablo (1974)
Portrait of Evil (1975)
Beyond the Dark (1978)

Non-Fiction

The New Crime Book (1972; with Richard Posner)

Black Gat Books

Black Gat Books is a new line of mass market paperbacks introduced in 2015 by Stark House Press. New titles appear every other month, featuring the best in crime fiction reprints. Each book is size to 4.25" x 7", just like they used to be, and priced at $9.99. Collect them all.

Stark House Press

1315 H Street, Eureka, CA 95501 707-498-3135 griffinskye3@sbcglobal.net www.starkhousepress.com
Available from your local bookstore or direct from the publisher.

Made in the USA
Monee, IL
15 April 2021